ALONG THE WAY

A Bicycle Odyssey

Jake Jacobson

Based on a cross country trip
by the author

iUniverse, Inc.
Bloomington

Along the Way
A Bicycle Odyssey

This is a work of fiction. All of the characters, names, incidents, organizations, and dialogue in this novel are either the products of the author's imagination or are used fictitiously.

iUniverse books may be ordered through booksellers or by contacting:

iUniverse
1663 Liberty Drive
Bloomington, IN 47403
www.iuniverse.com
1-800-Authors (1-800-288-4677)

ISBN: 978-1-4502-5293-5 (sc)
ISBN: 978-1-4502-5292-8 (e-b)

Printed in the United States of America

iUniverse rev. date: 11/10/2010

To Kris, my loving wife
Her encouragement helped
me to finish this book.

TABLE OF CONTENTS

Back in the USA

Appendix

A Wild Hair

WHEN WE WOKE UP, the sun was shining brightly. The bags were packed, the bikes were leaning against the wall, and after we strapped on the sleeping bags, we would be ready to go. We had quit our jobs, sold the cars, put our household goods in storage, and it was the last day of the lease on our apartment. For the past year, we had been planning and training for the incredible odyssey that lay ahead of us. We were going to ride our bicycles from Portland, Oregon to Portland, Maine.

It all started when Kris and I came back from a short bike ride. I was sitting in the living room, reading a magazine article about a cross-country bicycle trip. In the early 1970's, in preparation for the 1976 United States Bicentennial, a group of people collaborated to create a new coast-to-coast bicycle route from Virginia to Oregon. They installed signs, published maps, and called it the *Bike*centennial Trail. Then, in the summer of 1976, more than four thousand people made that trip on their bikes.

As I read on, some of the people were describing their trip. They talked about how amazing it had been to see the country from the seat of their bikes. I thought that maybe Kris would like to hear about this. When I went into the kitchen, she was in the middle of fixing dinner.

"Krissy," I said, "I've just been reading this article about …"

"Not right now," she interrupted. "I'm really kind of busy. Just put it on the coffee table and I'll read it later."

I guess I should have picked a better time to tell her about it. I went back into the living room and continued reading. That article got me to thinking, and my *wild hair* started to take shape!

Imagine all the things those people saw along the way. They must have had quite an adventure, and I wondered what it must have been like. Then I started wondering if *we* could make a trip like that! Just think, the two of us cruising down the highway on our bikes, on our way to the east coast.

When I got to thinking about it, my wild hair seemed a little far-fetched. We had a hard time just riding across town. Still, the whole thing was starting to grow on me.

After I finished washing the dinner dishes, I found Kris reading that article.

"Is this the article you were talking about before dinner?" she asked.

"That's the one," I said.

"Hmm," she said, "their trip sounds kind of interesting."

Well, if she found it interesting, maybe I should tell her about my idea.

"Honey," I said, "I just came up with this wild hair. We both love to travel, so what would you think about doing that trip in reverse?"

"Well," she said, "that's an intriguing idea. But I don't know if I really want to drive across the country. But, if we did, I would definitely want to take my Cadillac. It's way more comfy than your little sports car. So, how long do you think a trip like this would take?"

"Honey … uh … sweetie," I stammered. "I was not thinking about making that trip in a car. I was thinking about doing it on our bikes."

The silence was deafening. She slowly turned to me and asked, "Come on, Jake, you can't be serious? Did you say we should make that trip on our bicycles? Have you taken leave of your senses? We both have jobs, cars, and a house full of furniture. Am I supposed to go tell my boss that I'm taking some time off, so my husband and I can go gallivanting across the country on our bicycles? That's just nuts."

When she put it like that, it did sound kind of nuts. Kris had a good job as a lab-tech at one of the local hospitals. She had been there for several years, and she really liked her work. I understood how she felt, because I also enjoyed my job as a designer for a manufacturing company. Our friends often told us how lucky we were to have found some type of work that we really liked. For most of them, it was just a paycheck.

But, I could not leave it alone. "Now wait a minute," I replied. "Before you say no, think about this. You and I could see the country as few people have ever been able to. Can you imagine what an adventure that would be?"

"Oh yeah, right," she said, "a real adventure. You must have gotten too much sun today, because you are not making much sense."

She just shook her head and left the room. However, I could not get the idea out of my head. One evening, as we sat down to dinner, I brought it up again.

"Honey," I said, "I re-read that article about the cross-country bike trip, and I got all excited again. I really think that my wild hair would be a great adventure."

She seemed rather frustrated when she said, "Would you please just get over it, and forget about that strange idea! I have no desire to ride across the country. Our weekend rides are fun, but that is as far as it goes. Besides, we have our jobs to consider, and I'm *not* going to give mine up."

Well, that seemed quite definite. I figured that my wild hair was now a dead issue.

About a month later, as we sat down to dinner, Kris looked over at me and said, "I've just been thinking about that wild hair you had, the one about riding across the country. That's the craziest notion you've ever come up with."

"Yes," I said, "I do come up with some oddballs, don't I? But that one was kind of stupid. After all, we have trouble just riding across town. Just forget I even mentioned it."

"But that's the problem," she said. "I have not been able to get that *stupid idea* out of my head." She broke into a grin as she continued, "I dug out that article about the Bikecentennial ride and read it through a couple of times. I discovered what got you so fired up. The idea of you and me riding together across the country really does sound exciting." After a slight pause, she looked at me and said, "I may be totally out of my mind, but I think we should do it!"

What had I just heard? "Honey," I said, "did you just say that we should make that bike trip? Is that what I heard?"

She came around the table, gave me a big hug and answered "*Yes! Yes! Yes!* That is absolutely what you heard."

"Wow!" I said, "Do you mean my wild hair might actually become a reality?"

"Yes, you big oaf," she responded. "Your wild hair will definitely become a reality!"

As I stood there, being overwhelmed by what had just transpired, a multitude of questions poured into my head. What about our jobs, and our cars, and the furniture? And how would we get ready for such an undertaking? And, and, and …

Preparations

Planning the Trip

As the magnitude of Kris's startling revelation sank in, I realized we had a lot to discuss.

"Honey," I said, "several weeks ago you said that you had no desire to ride across the country. You also said that there was no way you would give up your job. Now, all of a sudden, you are ready to do just that. What happened to change your mind?"

"As I said," she replied, "after reading that article several times, I discovered what got *you* so excited about the possibility of making this trip. You were absolutely right about it being an amazing *adventure*, and I got excited about the two of us sharing that adventure. I just never considered doing it on bicycles."

"But," she continued, "there was one more thing bothering me. I was really concerned about giving up my job. So, I approached my boss about the possibility of getting my job back if we were to make this trip. He told me that he really did not want to see me leave. But, if I absolutely had to make this trip, he would have a spot for me when I returned. Wow, was that a relief! It felt as if a weight had been lifted, because I was really beginning to get excited. So, how about *you?*" she asked. "Do you still want to make the trip?"

"Are you referring to the funk I've been in for the last couple of weeks?" I asked. "Of *course* I still want to make the trip. What you told me at dinner really caught me by surprise, and I couldn't be happier. So, does that mean we are *both* committed?"

"That means we are both definitely committed," she assured me.

"Wow," I replied, "what a turn-around. Several weeks ago it was a dead issue, and now it appears that my wild hair is going to become a reality. So, I guess the first item on the agenda would be to figure out *when* we want to do this?"

"I've been thinking about that," Kris said, "and I have a plan, as usual. How about doing this next summer, in 1980? That will give us more than a year to prepare, and get all of our miscellaneous details in order. Then we could start the next decade with a real bang."

"You certainly have been thinking about it," I said. "I like that idea of starting the next decade with a bang."

After several discussions, we finally agreed that we should start the trip on June 1, 1980. Hallelujah! One item scratched off the list and about a thousand more to go. Next on the agenda was *what route to take*? It was quite obvious to me that we should ride the Bikecentennial Trail.

"You know," I said, "if we took the Bikecentennial route, we could get lots of information. There are maps already published, the trail is marked with signposts, and we could get pointers from people who have already made the trip,"

But, Kris had other ideas.

"Well, here are my thoughts on that," she began. "I really don't want to go where thousands of people have gone before. Why don't we figure out our own route? That way it will be *our* adventure, and not a repeat of what other people have experienced."

We had several more discussions about what route to take. I was stuck on the Bikecentennial Trail, and she was convinced that we should take a completely new route. Try as I might, I could not convince her that my way was better. I finally gave in and said bye-bye to the Bikecentennial Trail.

To begin figuring out our new route, we spread out a map of the USA on the kitchen table. Okay, there was Portland, Oregon on the west coast. Now where on the east coast did we want to wind up? I suggested New York City, but Kris replied there was *no way* that she would go there. It was too big a city, with far too many cars buzzing around. Well, how about Atlantic City, where we could do some gambling once we got there? That was probably not such a good idea, as we could lose all our money and be stuck there. I suggested Yorktown, Virginia, on the coast. (It's actually the starting place of the Bikecentennial Trail). I thought I was being a bit sneaky, but Kris put a quick stop to that notion. She had actually looked up the Bikecentennial Trail and found out that Yorktown was the east end of the trail. Okay, okay, so how about Boston? Nah, that's just another big city with too much traffic.

We kept looking until Kris spotted something.

"Are you kidding me?" she said. "I forgot that there were two of them."

"What are you talking about?" I asked. "There are two of what?"

"There are two cities named Portland," she replied. "One is right here in Oregon, and the other is in Maine. It is exactly what we have been looking for. We could call our trip *Portland to Portland*. What do you think?"

"That's right, there is a Portland in Maine," I exclaimed. "I think Portland to Portland has a *great* ring to it. Shall we call Portland, Maine our destination?"

After an exuberant yell, we did a little jig around the kitchen table and broke out a bottle of wine to celebrate.

So, what next? Well, we took our USA map and drew a straight line between the two Portlands. Oops. There were not any roads that ran like that. But do you know what? That line showed us what states we might be going through. It was not such a bad idea after all.

As we continued to study the map, it occurred to us that we might have to do something different when we got to the Great Lakes. Our line ran right through a couple of them, and we wouldn't be carrying any pontoons for the bikes. So, should we ride south around the Great Lakes, and go through the heavy industrial areas in Chicago, Indiana, and Ohio? Talk about big cities and heavy traffic! That's a big *no*! Then we would have to go north, which would put us into Canada. We kind of liked that idea. Of course, they would know right off that we were Yanks when we did not end every phrase with "eh."

So, back to the basic question: how do we get from here to there? First, we would ride through Oregon. (Now there's a real flash of brilliance, since our starting point would be in Oregon.) There would definitely be some mountains to cross, like the Cascade Range, the Blue Mountains, and who knows what else.

Then we could ride on into Idaho, which has the Rocky Mountains. I really did not like the idea of having to climb all those mountains. Maybe we could go around them? Oh sure, we would have to ride down into Arizona to get around them. I think not!

Next, Kris suggested going to the northeast corner of Idaho to Yellowstone National Park, the home of the Old Faithful geyser. That sounded good to me, since I had never been to Yellowstone. So, where should we go after Yellowstone?

General George Custer's famous last stand took place at the Little Big Horn in Montana, and that was something we both really wanted to see. According to our maps, US Hwy 212 would take us out of the northeast exit of Yellowstone and on into Montana to the Little Big Horn. Good plan!

From there it would be a fairly straight shot to South Dakota. Kris mentioned that she had never seen Mt Rushmore, the famous mountain sculpture of four presidents, and neither had I. It sounded as if we might have to park the bikes, rent a car, and take a little side trip. After that, we could head north to visit some friends in North Dakota.

From there we could head east into Minnesota and visit my brother in Minneapolis. But I thought that we had decided to stay away from large cities. Isn't Minneapolis a big city? Yes it is, but we would just have to make this one exception.

From there we thought we would head on into Wisconsin, where I grew up, to visit my family for a few days. After leaving my family, we would ride north through the Upper Peninsula of Michigan and on into Canada.

We would then ride around the north side of the Great Lakes in Canada, and drop back down into the USA in upstate New York. Continuing on east through New York, Vermont, and New Hampshire, we would finally finish up in Portland, Maine.

Hey, so much for planning the route, right? Well, not exactly; we were just getting started. Next we had to get detailed state maps and figure out which roads we were actually going to take. So, how about the Interstate Highways, they were pretty straight with nice broad shoulders. What do you mean we can't ride our bicycles on the Interstate? Unfortunately, that is correct. Evidently the lawmakers do not consider it safe to have bicycles on them, even with the wide shoulders. We would just have to stick to the regular state highways.

Next we had to decide how far we should plan to ride each day. Forty miles? Fifty miles?? Sixty miles??? We kicked that around for several days before we came to a conclusion. Our final compromise was between fifty and sixty miles per day. That seemed like a good pace if we planned to get to the east coast in a reasonable amount of time. Riding that many miles *every day* meant that we would need to do some training. Perhaps I should say a *lot* of training.

Figuring out our route was a very tedious task, which took us the better part of six months to complete. Since we were members of AAA, we went to the local office and picked up a stack of campground guidebooks, one for each state, to figure out where we were going to camp each night. That also gave us a specific destination for each day's ride.

Okay, the route planning was complete, but it was definitely subject to change.

Next on the agenda was the budget. How much would this adventure cost, and how would we finance it? After much discussion, and some number-crunching, we estimated that the cost for food and camping, with an occasional motel thrown in, should come to about … four thousand dollars? Are you serious? Wow, it looked like we would need to start saving our shekels.

We really did not want to go out on the road with that much cash in our pockets. So, I suggested that we set up accounts at banks along the way. That way we could stop by the bank, get our money, and be on our way. Once again, Kris had a different idea.

"Listen to this" she said. "We could set up an account here with my friend Sandy as a co-signer. Then, when we need some money, we could call her and she could mail it to us."

"Oh sure, she just mails it to us?" I asked. "What do you suppose she would use for an address? Remember, we'll be traveling across the country with no address." I thought she had lost it.

"Wait, I wasn't finished" she replied. "When we call her, we would tell her where we were going to be in a few days, and she could send it to that Post Office in care of General Delivery. Then she would call the Post Office, let them know that we were on our way, and ask them to hold the letter for us. When we got there, we would show our ID and pick up the letter."

I was stunned! She had really thought this through, and had obviously done some research. "Honey," I said, "you've done it again. That is a great idea, I really like it. Shall we talk to Sandy?"

"Oh, yeah," she said. "Well, I've already done that. She said she would be happy to help us out."

As usual, she was way ahead of me!

So, the planning was done. But, what were we going to do about those bikes?

The Bikes

When Kris and I first started cycling, we purchased used bikes from the newspaper. They were old and heavy, so we called them our tanks. Even though they were not a perfect fit, they worked well for short weekend rides. Long before coming up with my wild hair, we enrolled in a bicycle maintenance class. We wanted to know what to do if we ran into trouble, like changing a flat or replacing a broken spoke. Little did we know how important that class would be later on.

Whenever we took the tanks to a bike shop, the mechanics would always tell us that they were old, heavy, and probably not worth what we were putting into them. However, we could not justify putting out money for new bikes, because the tanks suited our needs.

When the idea of the trip came along, we needed to reconsider what we would be riding. The tanks would definitely *not* be making the trip. So what were we going to ride? We decided to go visit our favorite bike shop to get some advice from the experts.

The owner, Bob, came over to help us. We told him about our wild hair, and that we needed some help. He took a look at the tanks that we had ridden to the shop, and agreed that they should not make the trip. He measured both of us to see what they might have in the shop. It turned out that Kris could get away with just about any standard model. Then he turned to me.

"You, young man," he said, "are a mess." Bob could see I was not too fond of *that* remark. He went on, "Sorry, Jake, that was not meant as an insult. It's just that you have a long torso and short legs." (Do you suppose that was news to me?) "Most bikes are built in proportion to height and length. You have the torso for a longer bike, but with your short legs, you would need to have a shorter frame. I'm afraid I don't have anything like that. Oh, we have a few that you could use for short rides, and possibly for training. But you would be miserably cramped after a few days on the road."

"I have another problem," I told him. "Those narrow seats tend to make my behind sore, and then my groin goes numb. Do you have any idea how to remedy that situation?"

Bob stood there thinking for a moment. "It could be just a matter of getting your seat adjusted properly," he said. "But, we may have another solution for you. Just wait here and I'll be right back." He returned a few minutes later with Carl, one of his mechanics.

After listening to our story, Carl said, "I would recommend you get custom-built frames. That's probably the only way Jake is going to get something to fit."

"Okay," I said, "so where would we go for that?"

"Just south of town there's an excellent builder that we've worked with before," Carl said. "He could set you up with frames to fit your measurements." When I told him about my butt problem, he said, "I think he may have a solution. He's building a new type of bike called a recumbent."

"What in the world is a recumbent?" I asked.

"It's kind of hard to describe," Carl replied. "Let me draw a sketch for you."

His sketch showed a low, stretched-out bike, with a chair-like seat that sat much lower than a standard bicycle seat. The pedals were situated in front of the rider instead of underneath, and the front wheel was smaller than the rear.

I leaned over and whispered to Kris, "That thing looks kind of weird!"

"Really?" she replied. "I think it looks rather interesting."

"So," I asked, "how would this thing solve my problem?"

Carl turned to Bob and asked if he could use one of his office chairs. Bob wandered off and came back pushing an office chair.

"Have a seat," Bob said, so I sat in the chair.

Carl placed a box in front of me and said, "Now, lean back and put your feet up on the edge of the box." When I did so, he asked, "How does that feel?"

"It feels pretty good," I replied, "but, what is this all about?"

Carl replied, "This is just to show you how a recumbent bicycle feels. It has a seat much like this office chair, and the box is about where the pedals would be."

"Well," I said, "this is very comfy, but I still don't see how it would work. Does this builder have an actual, ah, what did you call it?"

"It's called a recumbent," Carl said, "and yes, he does have one that you can try out. It's comfortable, easy to ride, and I think it would solve your sore butt problem."

He wrote down the builder's address and phone number for us. When we left the shop, we were more confused than when we first arrived.

About a week after our visit to the bike shop, and a couple more sore butts, we had a discussion about the bikes. I was still kind of reluctant to go to the frame builder.

"Jake," Kris said, "this is crazy. I think you are afraid of what you might find, and you have stalled long enough. This morning I called that builder and made an appointment. We are going to check out that recumbent bicycle *now*!" She grabbed me by the arm, led me out to the car, and we went to see the builder.

When we pulled in, we were greeted by the wizard.

"Hi," he said, "my name is John. Welcome to my humble shop." He was a rather tall, soft-spoken man with rimless glasses and disheveled salt and pepper hair. He was wearing jeans, an orange t-shirt, and a brown leather apron.

"Hi, my name is Kris," she said, "and this is my husband Jake. I called this morning to make an appointment."

"Oh sure," he said as we shook hands, "been waiting for you. Come on in." Inside there were several tables with welding fixtures on them, a couple of welding torches, and parts of frames hanging from hooks on the walls. As I looked around, my curiosity got the better of me.

"John," I said, "what is with all those frame parts that are hanging on the walls?"

He just chuckled. "You are not the first one to ask that question. They are actually parts of frames that I am working on for other people."

Silly me, I had no idea how bike frames were built. I just assumed that all the tubes would be welded together at the same time.

"So, how can I help you?" he asked.

We told him about the trip we were planning, the old tanks we were riding, and that we needed something more appropriate to make the trip.

"A mechanic at the bike shop measured us," I said, "and told us that they had a number of models to fit Kris. But, because I have this rather weird body, with short legs and a long torso, they didn't have anything to fit me. Carl suggested that we see you about getting custom-built frames."

John replied, "I'll have to thank him when I see him again. Standard bikes, like those in a bike shop, are not designed for touring. They become kind of mushy when you add more weight, and the average bike tourist carries between thirty and forty pounds."

We didn't like the sound of that, and hoped he was wrong.

"I also have another problem," I continued. "Sitting on those narrow bicycle seats, my butt gets sore and then goes numb. Carl told us that you were building a new contraption that might solve my problem. He said it was called a recumbent."

John grinned and said, "Yes, I do build recumbents, and it might be just what you are looking for. Wait right here" He went to the back of his shop and came back with a recumbent, much like the sketch we had been shown at the bike store.

"How in the world did you come up with something like this?" I asked.

"Well, I was looking at a bicycle magazine," he said, "and there was an ad for a recumbent being sold in Massachusetts. I figured I could build one for a lot cheaper than what they wanted. After some tinkering, I finally came up with what you see here. I have already sold a few, and the customers have been totally thrilled."

It did look *something* like a bike, but it was longer and a lot lower than a standard bike. Plus, the wheels were not the same size. On the rear was a twenty-seven-inch wheel, and on the front was a smaller, twenty-inch wheel. It had a seat with a backrest, and the pedals were located out in front of the seat.

Once again, my curiosity got the best of me. "Could I sit on it," I asked, "to see how it feels?"

He held the bike for me as I sat down and put my feet on the pedals. I was surprised how comfy it felt. The bottom of the seat was padded, and it supported me very nicely. The backrest was made of a mesh material to keep your back from sweating. The brake handles and shifters were mounted on the handlebars, which were right in front of me.

"Honey," I said, "come sit on this thing. It's really comfy."

Kris sat down and her eyes got big. "Yeah, this is nice," she said.

"Okay, so it's very comfy," I said. "But, how does it ride?"

John said, "Let's go find out." We walked the bike out to the street and John held on to the seat as I sat down. "Now, just lean back against the seat," he told me, "and start pedaling."

As I did so, I started moving down the street. John still had hold of the seat and was running alongside to steady me. The balance was much different than that of a standard bike. When he let go, I started wobbling, and it felt like I was going to tip over. John yelled at me to lean back and keep pedaling. I did that, and I finally got the feel of the balance. The wobbles started to go away, and pretty soon I was riding fairly straight. At the next intersection I made a big circle and rode back to the shop. As I pulled back into the driveway, I had a huge grin on my face.

Kris came running over and said, "Okay, my turn." She sat down and John gave her the same running start. When he let go, Kris wobbled a couple times, stopped pedaling, and fell over. Ouch!

"You have to lean back and keep pedaling," John told her, and they started over again.

She made half a dozen attempts, but each time she fell over. I could see that Kris was getting frustrated, so I told John to stop. When she came over to me, I gave her a big hug.

"Honey," she said, "I really wanted to ride that thing, but I just could not get it to work."

"It's okay," I said. "We'll just go back to the standard bicycles."

"Whoa," John said. "Let's not give up so quickly. I have been experimenting with something that may be just what the doctor ordered. I'll be right back. "

He went back into his shop, and came out with a three-wheeled version of what we had just been trying out. It had twenty-inch wheels all around, with one in the front and two in the back. I could see that the rear end was completely different, in order to accommodate the two wheels.

When Kris saw it, she smiled at me and said, "That's more like it. I can ride that one!"

John adjusted the seat and took her out to the street. As she sat down and started pedaling, her eyes lit up. When she returned, she was grinning from ear to ear. "Now, this is what I call a terrific ride," she said. "I don't have to worry about falling over."

That got a chuckle out of John. "Why don't you two take them around the block," he said, "so you can get a better idea of how they feel?"

He started to walk over to help me get started.

"No, wait," I said. "Just tell me how to do it."

"Okay," he said. "First of all, lean back in the seat." I did that. "That way, you sort of become one with the bike, and you have more control. Now, I see that you put your right foot down when you stop. Rotate the pedals backward so that the left pedal is at the top." I did that. "That way, when you push against it, you will start moving. Don't try to scoot with your right foot, because you need to have it ready when the right pedal comes to the top. Then you can use your right foot to continue pedaling."

I tried his technique several times, and I was able to take right off.

"Okay," he said, "I think you've got it. Now, go for a ride."

As we pulled away from the shop, I was amazed how well his technique worked. It was as if I had been doing it forever. Kris, of course, had no problem at all. Before we got back to the shop, I stopped Kris to get her thoughts on these new bikes.

"So, what do you think?" I asked.

"This is so much nicer than any *bicycle* I've ever ridden," she replied. "How does your butt feel?"

"I have never had such a happy butt," I told her, "and the ride is so smooth."

She grinned at me and said, "Mine is pretty smooth, too. Should we go back and see about having John build a couple for us?"

"I don't know," I said. "Do you think we can afford them? They're really nice, but ..."

"Jake," Kris said, in kind of reprimanding way, "you're stalling again. Yes, we can afford them, and I think we should get them. Okay?"

"Well, when you put it like that," I said, "how can I say no? Okay, let's go give John the good news."

When we returned to the shop, we told John that we wanted to buy his amazing recumbents. He told us that we could have them in any color we wanted, and that he would deliver them, ready to ride, in a couple months. We went back into his shop, and he gave us a list of components, including racks, that he was going to use. He told us to call him if we wanted something different. Each bike would have one rack in the back, to hold two large bags, and two racks under the seat, to hold two smaller bags. He showed us the racks he would be using, and how they would mount, so that we could get the right bags.

When we got back home, we decided that we should take our list to the bike store. We were pretty sure John would not steer us wrong, but it never hurts to get a second opinion. Bob was just coming out of his office, so we grabbed him before someone else could.

"Hi Bob," I said. "We just came back from the frame builder that Carl suggested. We have decided to buy the recumbents. What a comfy, smooth ride."

Bob just chuckled, and said, "After we gave you that high-tech demonstration, I would have been surprised if you had *not* chosen them. So, what can I do for you?"

"Well," I said, "John gave us a list of components that he is going to supply with the bikes, but we don't know what's good and what's not. Could we pick your brains a bit?"

"Not a problem," Bob replied, "I'm going to turn you over to Carl. Whenever we have a question about components, we go to him." A couple minutes later Bob came walking back with Carl. Bob had explained our situation to him, and suggested we use the office.

As we were getting settled, Carl said, "So, you took my advice about the recumbents."

"Yes, those things are amazing," I replied.

"I had an idea you might like them," he said with a grin. "Now let's get down to business." He started looking over our list and making notes. When he got done, he wrote down a couple of alternatives that might work better for us.

Bob saw us come walking out of the office, with smiles on our faces. "Was Carl able to help you?" he asked.

"He certainly did." I said. "He said that most of the components on the list were really good choices, and he gave us a couple of alternative suggestions. So, now we have our final list, and we can't thank you enough."

"You can thank me," Bob said, "by coming back when you need work done, or to buy some new components."

"Well," I said, "I guess we may as well start thanking you right now. We need to buy some bags."

They had a very good selection, in several different colors. There were blue ones, red ones, and yellow ones. Kris really wanted red bags, but I mentioned that yellow would be a more noticeable color on the road. She kept insisting that she wanted red bags, so I reluctantly agreed. Red bags for her, but I was going to get the yellow bags. Both sets had a reflective strip sewn onto the rear panel, which would make them show up if we had to be on the road at night.

A couple days later we called John with our changes.

"Hey, what took you so long to get back to me?" he asked, and then broke out into a laugh. "I really didn't expect to hear from you so soon. Those changes are good ones, and should last you for a long time."

It would have been nice to have today's components back then. The click shifting, clipless pedals and braking systems that are used on today's bikes are far superior to what was available in the late 70's.

A couple months later, after returning from one of our sore butt rides, we had an exciting phone message. John had called to say that he would be delivering our bikes in a few days. We were almost beside ourselves with excitement when he arrived and pulled our gleaming new bikes from his van. My two-wheeler was green, Kris's three-wheeler was purple, and they were beautiful!

John showed us how to adjust the seats, and then suggested we take the bikes for a ride before he left. As we eased ourselves into the seats and turned the pedals, the bikes started to roll. We both let out a howl of delight. We just rode around the parking lot, but it was enough to realize that we had made a great decision. When we got back to the van, John pulled out our new racks and showed us how to mount them.

"Now," he said, "I've done something with the trike that might help on the trip. The left rear wheel is the drive wheel. Here's why that is important. If you come upon a stretch of road with no shoulder, Kris can ride beside the road with just her left rear wheel on the pavement. That way she can maintain traction, instead of spinning her wheel in the dirt."

"Wow," Kris said. "It seems like you have thought of everything. Thank you so much."

"You're very welcome," John said. "That's about all I have to tell you about your bikes. If you run into any problems, or have any questions, give me a call." After we shook hands, he climbed back into his van and left.

When John drove out of sight, we did a little jig and took our new bikes for a ride. That initial ride was not very long, maybe a couple of miles, but everything worked great, just as we had hoped it would.

When we pulled back into the parking lot, I yelled, "Bring it on, we are ready for the open road!"

But we were far from ready. We still had a lot of *stuff* to take care of.

And Stuff

Have you ever tried to figure out what to pack if you'll be gone for several months? Well, neither had we. As it turned out, clothes would not be that big of a problem. During the day, we'd be wearing shorts and t-shirts. After we stopped for the day, we would probably change into sweats. If we wanted to go someplace nice for dinner, we could take along slacks and a pullover shirt. Of course, we would also have to include socks and underwear, which we almost left off the list. (Just another one of those things you often take for granted.)

Next on the list were the non-clothing items. That included such things as cooking gear, a tent, sleeping bags, and rain gear. A friend of ours suggested that we could probably find what we needed at a backpacking equipment store. When we got there, we thought we had discovered a gold mine. We found lightweight camping and cooking gear that was designed for backpacking. A young lady, who we later discovered was an experienced backpacker, came over to help us.

"Hi," she said. "My name is Ashley. How can I help you?"

"Well," I began, "we really don't know where to start. We have decided to go on a long bicycle trip, and we need help getting outfitted."

"Did I hear you correctly, that you will be on bicycles?" she asked.

"That's right," I said, "we'll be on bicycles."

"Where are you headed?" she asked.

Kris piped up with "Portland, Maine."

"You're going to ride your bicycles from here to Portland, *Maine*?" Ashley asked. "Wow, I would call that a very ambitious endeavor. I'm sure there's a story to go along with that, but, let's see about getting you set up with some good equipment. What do you have so far?"

"Would you believe nothing?" Kris replied.

Ashley sort of grinned and said, "Oh my, I think we may be in for a long afternoon. First off, let me give you a little background about myself. I started hiking and backpacking with my father when I was fifteen. I liked it so much, I couldn't stop. That was fifteen years ago. I started selling the equipment about five years ago, and have gone through all the training that the store provides. Most of the equipment in here has been used by the staff at one time or another."

At that point I happened to get a good look at Ashley's name tag. It said, "Assistant Store Manager." We were in good hands.

"Will you be camping on your trip?" she asked. "By that, I mean will you be carrying cooking gear, tents, and sleeping bags with you?"

Kris took over at this point. "I believe that would be yes to all of the above. I will probably be doing all the cooking, just like I do at home."

She and Ashley had a good chuckle over that one. Yeah, she did the cooking and I washed the dishes. Isn't that the way it works in most households?

"So, show me how this stuff works" Kris said.

Ashley showed us some small aluminum cookware sets that stowed inside of one another. To use the cookware, we would need some kind of stove. She showed us a number of small, single-burner white-gas stoves. The one Ashley suggested, and the one we bought, came apart for easy cleaning and storage. The burner unit looked like a smaller version of one of the burner units on a gas range in your kitchen, and it had its own storage bag. It screwed on to the top of a fuel canister, which was about four inches in diameter and about three inches high. The canister also had three small legs that folded up when you were done cooking, and it had its own storage bag. When you were through, you could empty the gas back into an aluminum container about the size of a water bottle with a sealed top.

Another item on the list was tents.

"Would you like to look at some small, very lightweight, single-person tents?" she asked. "That way you could each carry your own tent."

"That might be nice for a single person," Kris replied, "but I think we would like to look at some two-person tents. We like to snuggle."

Ashley chuckled and said, "Okay, let's look at the two-person tents. Some are nice and light, but not that easy to set up and take down. The one I would recommend is this one over here."

They had several different tents set up on display, and she pointed out a green tent. "This one is self-contained," she said, "meaning that you can pick up the whole thing and move it around without it coming apart. All you have to do is stake down the corners to hold it in place. Plus, it is easy to break down, and it all fits into a nice, small, carrying bag."

"That looks like it is exactly what we're looking for." I said. "So, what about sleeping bags?"

Ashley said, "You will probably want something light that would still be warm enough for the cool summer nights in the mountains." As she picked one up she said, "I used this particular bag when I was hiking in the mountains. A nice feature is that two of them can be zipped together to form a nice, warm, snuggly bag for the two of you. They also come with individual stuff sacks. Now, along with the sleeping bags, you will also want some mats to put under the bags. After all," she said, "you will be lying on the ground, and the mats will give you a little cushion."

Wow, those mats sounded like a great idea, so we took her up on the suggestion. The ones we bought were self-inflating to about two inches thick. You just had to open a valve and the air came rushing in. To deflate, you opened the valve and then squeezed out all the air. They also came with their own stuff sacks.

So, what if the weather gets nasty? Better check into some rain gear. (We had no idea that it would also turn into *snow* gear! You'll find out more about that later.)

Ashley took us over to their rain gear area and said, "If you are wearing rain gear while riding, you do *not* want to create a rain shower *inside* your clothing. That means the material has to be breathable, which would let the air through but keep the rain out. Most of it is kind of spendy, but worth the extra money."

She had us try on some that were soft and pliable, and not quite so spendy. We invested in matching bright yellow jackets and pants, and some waterproof high-top booties that we could slip on over our sneakers.

By the time we left the store, we had accumulated a lot of *stuff*. We put it all in our spare bedroom, along with everything else we were taking.

"Krissy," I said, "we've accumulated a lot of stuff here. Do you think it will all fit? Maybe we should leave the kitchen sink and the four-poster bed behind?"

"Oh no," she cried, "I was really looking forward to that four-poster bed. Ha-ha, real funny! I think we should have room for all of it. Those bags we bought are pretty big."

"Well, let's hope so. Now that we've got everything," I said, "shall we see if it will all fit?"

"Oh ye of little faith," Kris answered. "Okay, just to satisfy your doubts."

The next evening we started by putting clothing into plastic bags, for later on when we ran into that dreaded wet stuff. Once that was completed, we decided who would carry what. I wound up with the tent, and we split up the cooking supplies. One of Kris's smaller bags was set aside for her camera gear, and one of my smaller bags was reserved for food. To my surprise, everything did fit in the bags, and it all weighed in at about thirty-five pounds for each of us. I guess John, the bike builder, really knew what he was talking about.

Now what was that about food? Ah yes, that precious commodity used for energy. How much would we take along, and how would we replenish it? After some discussion it became apparent that we had several options.

We could eat all of our meals at restaurants and not have to carry any food at all. On the other hand, we could cook all of our meals and have to frequently replenish our supplies. Carrying enough food for all of our meals would mean adding a lot of weight to our load. There was another consideration to think about. Since we were going to stay away from cities, where would we get the food? It would probably be at convenience stores or small mom and pop stores. It looked to us like the best option would be a combination of eating out and cooking in.

Now that we knew we were going to be carrying around an extra thirty-five pounds, perhaps we should do some *training*.

Training

When we decided to make the trip, we knew that we would have to do a *lot* of riding to get ourselves in shape. We only drove the car if we needed to haul a lot of groceries, or to go to work. For short trips, or to a store down the street, we rode our bikes. On weekends, we would go for rides in the country.

One of our friends told us about a local bicycle club that had organized rides on the weekends. Perhaps there would be some people who could give us some pointers on how to prepare for our trip. So, the next Saturday we joined them.

By this time we had the new bikes, and we got some very odd looks when we arrived. Several people wandered over and gave our bikes the once over. One guy was giving them a very close inspection.

"Where in the world did you get these?" he asked. "I've seen them advertised in bike magazines, but have never seen one up close. Are they as comfy as the ads say they are?"

"*We* think they are," I replied. "Would you like to try it out?"

"I sure would," he said with a grin. "By the way, my name is Troy"

"Hi," I said, "my name is Jake, and this is my wife, Kris."

"Here, sit on my trike," Kris said.

Troy thanked her, and sat down very carefully. He wiggled around a bit and settled back into the seat.

"Wow, this is nice," he said. "Is it difficult to ride?"

"Not mine," Kris said, "but Jake's is a little different."

"The balance on mine is different than a standard bike," I said, "so it takes a little getting used to. Would you like to try it?"

"Are you sure?" he asked. "I'd hate to tip it over and scratch it."

"Why don't you try mine," Kris said. "You won't have to worry about tipping it over."

As we wheeled the trike out to the street, a small crowd of onlookers followed us. I held it as Troy sat down and got situated.

"It's easier if you stay leaned back into the back rest," I said, "and just keep pedaling. So here we go."

I noticed that a grin come over his face as he started riding down the street. He went about fifty yards, turned around, and came riding back. The smile on his face told the whole story.

"Wow," he said, "that was amazing. What a nice smooth ride."

Several other people wanted to sit on it, so we obliged them. They all remarked about how comfortable it was.

About that time, the ride leader signaled us that the ride was about to begin. They were handing out maps for a thirty-mile ride or a fifty-mile ride. We opted for the thirty-mile ride. It was going to be out in the country, and it involved a number of hills. We all started the ride together, and right away you could tell who the stronger riders were. By the time we had covered a couple of miles, they had disappeared from sight. There was another group of riders who chose to start a little slower, and we attempted to stay with them. By the time we had covered ten miles Kris and I were by ourselves, bringing up the rear. We went on to finish, but it was pretty obvious that we were not in the same class as the rest of the group.

A couple days later we showed up on the doorstep of our favorite bike shop for advice. One of the mechanics came over and introduced himself.

"Hi," he said, "my name is Dave. I saw you two on that ride last Saturday, it's pretty hard to miss those recumbents. How did you do?"

"Hi, Dave," I said. "It was fun for about the first fifteen minutes. After that, we got left in the dust, when everyone just rode away from us."

"Was that your first club ride?" he asked.

"It was," Kris said, "and probably our last. It was pretty discouraging."

"I can imagine it was," Dave said. "But, try not to let it get you down. Most of those people have been riding for quite some time, and a number of them are racers."

Perhaps there was a lesson here. No matter what you attempt to do, there will always be those who do it better. They may have skills that you have yet to learn. Just do the best that *you* can.

"So, Dave," I asked, "what do we need to do to become better riders?"

"You need to attend a novice class that we are putting on next Saturday," Dave replied. He gave us a brochure that had all the information as to time and place.

The class was being held at a church, with a large parking lot, and there were half a dozen people there. Evidently, we were not the only ones who wanted to learn how to become better riders. Of course, they were all abuzz about our bikes. Everyone wanted to sit on them to see how comfy they were.

"So, where did you come up with these things?" someone asked.

We told them about John, and I figured he was about to get some new customers.

As we were entered the church, a lady told us to bring our bikes inside. When she saw us, she came over and introduced herself.

"Hi," she said, "my name is Marie. You two were at the club ride last week, right? I recognize the recumbents."

"Yes, we were," I said. "That ride really showed us that we have a lot to learn. So, here we are."

"Well," she said, "I think you are going to learn a lot. It looks like everyone is ready, so let's get started."

As she stepped up to the front, she said, "Hi, everyone, my name is Marie. I've been involved with racing for about five years, and I'll try to give you the benefit of what I've learned from my riding coach. This gentleman here," she said, as she put her hand on his shoulder, "is Phil, and he is a mechanic at a local bike shop."

Phil stepped up and said, "Good morning. First off, I'm going to discuss the kind of bikes we are riding, and how they fit us."

"Older bikes," he said, "are most likely going to be heavier, and therefore slower. Most of the newer bikes are lighter, more responsive, and easier to ride. And then there are recumbents. I don't have a clue how they ride."

Everyone turned to us and chuckled over that last remark.

"Regardless of whether it's old, new, or recumbent" he continued, "the fit of the bike is critical. If the bike is too short, from saddle to handlebars, you will be cramped up. If it is too long, you will be stretched out. In either case, you will probably become fatigued quickly, and not enjoy the ride."

"The next part of getting your bike to fit properly," he said, "is the correct distance from the saddle to the pedals. When the pedal is at the bottom of the stroke, with the ball of your foot on the pedal, you should still have a slight bend in your knee. We're going to take some time to come around and make sure everyone's bike is adjusted properly."

As they went around, they had everyone sit on their bikes, and then adjusted the seat height. When they got to us, Phil scratched his head, and had us sit on our bikes.

"Wow, recumbents. I've never seen one in person before," he said, "but I guess the adjustments would be about the same as on the standard bikes. If the seats are too far forward, you'll be cramped up. But, if they're too far back, you'll have to stretch for the pedals. However, it looks like someone has already set them up properly for you."

Phil hesitated for a moment, and then asked, "Would you mind if I sat on it? I just want to see how it feels."

"Here, try mine," Kris replied. "You won't have to balance it."

Phil straddled the trike and gingerly settled into the seat. A big smile came over his face and he started to chuckle.

"Oh man," he said, "this thing is really nice. After we finish, could I take it for a ride?"

"Absolutely," Kris said, "but shouldn't we get back to the class?"

"Oh, right, the class," he said as he got up. "Sorry folks, I kinda got distracted."

The rest of the people in the class were chuckling, as they had already had their shot at sitting on our bikes.

Marie took over on the next subject of *how* to ride. "As I said before, my name is Marie, and I'm going to talk about the speed at which you turn the pedals," she said. "That's called your cadence. Most beginning riders tend to use a cadence that is too slow, and hurt their knees by pushing the pedals, instead of spinning. We recommend that you use a cadence of between sixty to eighty revolutions per minute. Some racers use a cadence of ninety or more. I don't recommend that for you folks. Find something that's comfortable for you."

"In order to maintain proper cadence," she said, "you need to use your gearing effectively. When going up hills, shift into a lower gear. That means using a smaller front chain ring, or a larger rear sprocket. You will be riding slower, but you can still maintain your cadence. When going downhill, either coast or shift to a higher gear, a larger chain ring or a smaller rear sprocket. On level ground, choose a suitable gear to maintain your cadence and speed."

"The next subject," Marie continued, "is proper pedaling technique. That is, keeping a smooth rhythm as you turn the pedals. Let's go outside, so I can demonstrate what I mean."

After she got on her bike and started riding around the large parking lot, we were all pretty impressed at how smooth she was. When I looked at her head, there was hardly any movement, but she was pedaling very fast.

At this point, Phil took over again. "In order to be smooth, like Marie," he said, "you have to pull up with one foot, while pushing down with the other. It also means that you may need to use toe-clips, as Marie is doing, to keep your feet attached to the pedals."

Toe-clips are u-shaped pieces of metal that attach to the front of the pedals and then curl up over the toe of your shoe. There is also a strap that goes through some slots on the underside of the pedal, up around your foot, through a loop on the u-shaped metal piece, and then buckles into the other end of the strap.

Today, fewer people are using toe-clips. Instead, many riders today use what are called "clipless" pedals. They wear special shoes, with a cleat attached to the bottom of the shoe, which clicks into a matching cleat built into the pedal. By twisting your foot slightly, it unlocks your foot from the pedal.

I switched to clipless pedals a few years ago. In fact, I still remember my first ride with those things. I was participating in a club ride, and came upon a couple of friends who had stopped for a break and I decided to join them. As my bike came to a stop I tried to get my feet out of the toe-clips and couldn't. That's because I was using clipless pedals, not toe-clips.

On an old TV show called *Laugh-In*, there was a guy who would ride around on a kid's tricycle. Occasionally, he would run into something, or someone, and tip over sideways, while seated on the trike. Well, guess what happened? Because I could not get my feet free, I tipped over sideways while still seated on my bike, just like the guy on *Laugh-In*. I had forgotten to twist my feet, to release the pedals, before coming to a stop. My friends were laughing hysterically! One of them was even yelling, "*Laugh- In, Laugh-In!*"

(Oops, I got off on a tangent there; back to pedaling technique.)

After the class, Kris and I started reading everything we could find about pedaling technique. However, they all said about the same thing that Phil told us in class. We found out that reading about proper technique and actually doing it were two entirely different things. Even with toe-clips, which we used for the entire trip, it took us quite a while to get the hang of that technique. Once we got it figured out, we were pumped. We figured that we'd be riding just like those club riders.

A couple weeks later, we went on one of our Saturday rides. The recumbents were like riding on a cloud. It was time for a break when I saw a sign for a winery just a mile away. When we got there, we were greeted by the owners and given a tour. Of course we had to sample their various vintages.

That did not turn out to be such a good idea. We had not eaten since breakfast, and the wine went straight to our heads. The lady showing us around, her name was June, noticed our condition and quickly brought out some bread and cheese for us to munch on. They had some tables and chairs set up, which we made use of right away. June brought out some water and sat down with us.

"What kind of bikes are those?" she asked. "I have never seen anything like them."

"They're something pretty new called recumbent bicycles," I replied. "We are planning on taking a long bike trip, and we needed something that would be comfy for the trip. A local bike shop told us about this guy who makes them. He designed and built them for us, and we just love them."

"So, are they really comfortable?" June asked.

Kris replied, "Indeed they are, would you like to check them out?"

They went over to the trike, and June sat down rather carefully.

"Wow!" she exclaimed. "This really is comfy. I can see why you like them." When they came back over to the table, June asked, "Where are you planning to go on this trip?"

Kris answered, "We are planning to ride to Portland, Maine."

June's mouth dropped open, and she stammered a bit before she replied, "Did you say Portland, *Maine?*"

"Yes indeed," I said, "Portland, Maine." I went on to explain about the magazine article that had triggered the whole idea of the trip. June was just enthralled, and hung on our every word.

After about an hour of chatting about our upcoming trip, and about the vineyard, we sobered up. June wished us good luck as we got back on our bikes and headed for home.

We were quite tired by the time we arrived at our apartment. Kris checked her mileage computer to discover that we had ridden fifty-three miles. No wonder we were tired! It was the first of many fifty-plus mile rides in the months to come.

From that point on, we went out almost every weekend to do our training rides. We chose nice country roads that were not too hilly, so that we could get our miles in. Neither one of us liked climbing hills, so we avoided them like the plague. Our goal to begin with was to put in thirty to thirty-five miles on both Saturday and Sunday. We struggled with that at first, but after a while we were able to accomplish it quite easily, and pushed it up to fifty miles each day. Hmmm, not quite so easy, but we were still able to put in the miles on those easy country roads.

One night, while doing some route planning for the trip, we both noticed something about our route. We were going to be crossing a number of *mountain ranges*! That meant we would be doing a lot of hill climbing, which was the one thing we had been avoiding. It looked like we would need to change our training strategy. Instead of avoiding hills, we decided to include them on every ride. After thinking about that situation for a bit, I came up with a brilliant solution. At least *I* thought it was brilliant. When I explained it to Kris, she thought it might have some merit.

The idea was to continue with the fifty-mile country rides on Saturday, and then on Sunday we could ride downtown and back. That may not sound very challenging, but here was the situation. We lived about eight miles from downtown, and the West Hills of Portland stood right in the middle of that stretch. (Well, not *exactly* in the middle.) The West Hills began rising right at the edge of downtown. From there it was about two miles or so to the summit, which was a considerable elevation gain above city center. The other six miles to our place was a more gradual downhill slope. So, going into town would not be too bad of a climb, with a nice fast descent into city center. But then, we would have to turn around and make that steep ascent to the summit, with a nice gradual descent to home.

The following weekend we decided to try out my scheme. The extended Saturday ride worked out pretty well. We rode sixty miles and were plenty tired when we got home, but not enough to hinder our Sunday ride downtown.

After breakfast we rode the eight miles to downtown. The grade to the summit of the West Hills was not too bad, and we were rewarded with a swift downhill coast into the city center. We wandered around a bit and had a light lunch before we decided to attack that climb to the summit and head back home.

Fortunately, the route we chose had some switchbacks, which made the grade less severe. Even so, we were not prepared for the grind up that hill. Just put it in your lowest gear and spin right up the hill, right? Well, that's what we thought. But, I could have walked faster than we were riding. We decided we still needed more training on hills before doing our Sunday ride again.

What we realized was that the more we rode, the stronger we would get. The stronger we got, the easier those hills would become. In order to get stronger, we decided to do some exercises. You know, stuff like push-ups, sit-ups (ouch), and half-squats. What are half-squats, you ask? Well, you only go half way down and come back up again. Sounds easy, right? How about doing it twenty or thirty times with a full milk jug in each hand!

For about the first week or so we had some very sore muscles from all those exercises. Well, we kept up the exercises and pretty soon the soreness went away. We soon fell into a routine of exercising every other day. With all the riding and workouts we noticed that our clothes were fitting differently. We were both losing some weight. Imagine that!

Both of us tried to get in some riding every day, but that was not always possible. There were things that tended to get in the way like work, sleep, grocery shopping, and paying the bills. When we did get around to our daily ride, we had several routes figured out that were about twenty miles or so.

Leave it to me to come up with another scheme. We lived about twelve miles from my workplace and eight miles from where Kris worked. One day I asked Kris, "Why don't we save wear and tear on the cars and ride to work? That way we'll be able to get in our daily ride."

Kris worked on the west side of town, so she had a rather easy commute. I, on the other hand, worked on the east side. In between home and work were a bridge and those pesky West Hills of Portland. Remember that Sunday ride we took downtown? Well, now I would have to face that climb every night after work. This could be another scheme that blew up in my face, or so I thought. It actually turned out to be a good thing. Now I would be forced to do the training on hills that I so desperately needed.

When I started riding to work, I had a rather odd experience. Some of those days I arrived at work soaking wet, from the rain. On other days, I arrived soaking wet from sweating. Fortunately, my workplace had a shower, which I gladly made good use of.

At first, I really had to force myself to get on that bike in the morning. But, as time went by, it got easier. Later on, I actually looked forward to those early morning rides. So it is with anything that you want or desire. The work involved in reaching your goal gets easier the more you do it.

All the extra riding I was doing began to show up on our weekend rides. Kris was having a hard time keeping up with me, so I had to back off a bit. However, that only lasted for a few weeks. How was I to know that she was taking a longer route to and from her work? She had also decided to add a couple hills to her ride. After several weeks, our weekend rides started to change. Kris was taking the lead and I had to work to keep up. Her modified weekday commutes were paying dividends.

One evening, while figuring out our ride for the weekend, we decided to try one of those club rides again. It was to be a 50-mile ride to a lake west of town and back. When Saturday rolled around, we were there at the starting location. Once again, our bikes got some odd looks. A couple people wandered over and asked how we liked "those things". We told them that they were really comfy and easy to ride. They gave us a nod and walked away. Perhaps they remembered us from the previous ride.

We really did not know what to expect from this ride. Would all of our training and workouts pay off for us? Could we keep up with the pack, or would we be left in the dust again? As it turned out, we were much different riders than when we originally tried to keep up with the rear of the pack. This time we were in the thick of things in the middle of the pack. We were actually enjoying the ride and the companionship of the other riders. Once they found out that we really could ride, we were accepted as equals.

Our training routine had changed quite a bit. We were doing longer rides (fifty to sixty miles) every Saturday and Sunday with full packs. The extra thirty-five pounds we were each carrying made quite a difference. We had to gear down a little and ride a little harder. But we soon adjusted to it, and were cruising along again. As the weeks and months flew by, we were getting more and more excited about our upcoming trip.

With just a few months left, we decided to make this a true coast-to-coast trip. Our destination was Portland, Maine, on the coast of the Atlantic, but Portland, Oregon is about 100 miles inland. Hmm, that does not make it coast to coast, does it? To remedy that, we decided to make one of our weekend rides that little jaunt from the Pacific Coast to Portland. So, one Friday evening, another couple drove us to the coast. The next morning, we took our bikes down to the beach, and we actually dipped our rear wheels into the surf of the Pacific Ocean. Then we said good-bye to our friends, and were on our way.

That day we actually got our first real experience of mountain riding with full packs, as we had to cross the Oregon Coast Range. As mountain ranges go, it is not very high, but it gave us a taste of spending considerable time riding in our very lowest and slowest gear.

That evening, after conquering the Coast Range, we stopped at a campground just outside of a small town, and set up our tent. We had practiced putting it up in our back yard a number of times, so that was no problem. Now, how about some food? Oops, we had totally spaced that little detail. We were just a mile or so from town, so Kris rode in while I stayed at the campsite. She was better at picking out something good to eat.

While she was gone, I laid out the sleeping bags and got the campsite squared away. When Kris got back, I had the small camp stove set up and we had our first feast on the road. After dinner, we cleaned things up a bit and decided to call it a day.

The next morning, we woke up to find a layer of dew covering all of our gear. Our bikes were wet, our bags were wet, and so was our tent. What a fiasco, having to deal with that wet tent. It took us quite a while to squeeze out the water, and stuff that wet tent back into its carrying bag. We were going to have to practice that some more before we left. The rest of the day was a pretty easy ride, with no more mountains to climb. When we got home, we celebrated having completed the first leg of our trip.

However, that little trip showed us that we were lacking one important item. We needed something to cover our bikes. So, we went to the nearest hardware store and picked up a small tarp and some bungee cords.

It was the middle of May, and our departure day was fast approaching. We had both given our thirty-day notices at our jobs, the cars had been sold, and our furniture was in storage. All the preparations were going great, or so we thought.

Mother Nature was about to throw us a *huge* curve. We had been hearing that Mount St. Helens, a dormant volcano about fifty miles north of us in Washington, was becoming very active. Every day we heard reports that there were puffs of steams coming from various points on the mountain. We were thinking that if it ever actually blew, we would be long gone. Well, think again!

On Sunday morning, May 18, 1980, at 8:32 a.m., a 5.1 magnitude earthquake shook the mountain. That caused a bulge of the north side of the mountain to break away, and created one of the largest landslides in recorded history. As the north face slid away, the trapped gases of the hot magma below exploded like a well-shaken bottle of champagne. In only three minutes the blast flattened 230 square miles of old growth forest, spreading out in a fan shape north of the mountain. It also removed more than 1,300 feet from the summit and swept away almost the entire north side of the mountain. The elevation of the mountain dropped from 9,677 feet to 8,363 feet.

That Sunday, I was at my favorite bike shop when someone came running in to say that the mountain had blown. We rushed outside to see an enormous mushroom cloud rising from the mountain, as if someone had dropped a nuclear bomb. According to later reports, the cloud rose to 80,000 feet in about fifteen minutes.

However, the cloud had started drifting east and north, so we were not in any danger. Hey, wait a minute; if that stuff goes too far, like into Idaho (which it did) or Montana (which it did), it would deposit volcanic ash right in the middle of our planned route! Bummer! Oh well, at least it was drifting away from us, and we would be free to start our trip.

Do you really think so? Well, Mount St. Helens was not quite finished. The following Saturday, a week before our planned departure, another ash cloud erupted and it drifted south, dumping lots of ash on Portland. That nasty stuff is as fine as talcum powder and as abrasive as sandpaper.

We had just taken off on a short ride when the ash started falling. When we realized what was happening, we turned around and headed for home, but the damage had already been done. That ash had gotten into our chains, gears, and bearings and they were really trashed. Can you imagine what it did to all the cars that were out that day, running their usual Saturday morning errands? As the ash continued to fall, a lot of cars came to a halt with seized-up engines. It was a mess!

Was our trip over before it started? Not hardly! There was still a week to go before our planned departure date. Since we now had no transportation, one of our neighbors helped us out by taking us to our favorite bike shop. We had to have all of the components replaced that had been trashed by the ash. While our bikes were being repaired, we spent most of our time back at home shoveling ash into large garbage bags.

By the end of the week, our bikes were ready to go, and so were we.

Across the USA

Oregon

On the morning of June 1, 1980, we loaded our sleeping bags, tossed the keys to the apartment on the counter, and locked the door behind us. As we rode away from the apartment, we were excited about finally being on our way to the greatest adventure of our lives.

Our destination for the first day was Salem, about forty miles south. We had gone about ten miles when we saw a deer feeding near the side of the road. We were almost upon him before he saw us and dashed back into the woods. That was the first of many wild animal sightings. The rest of the day went pretty much as expected, like one of our training rides. Only this day was much different, because we would not be going back home.

That evening, some of our friends drove down and met us for dinner. They had come to help us celebrate our first day on the road. Halfway through dinner, a guy named Rick decided to give us a toast.

"I can hardly believe you two are actually going to do this," he said. "But, since you are, here is to a wonderful journey, and may God keep you safe."

As we raised our glasses, I looked around to see tears in the eyes of our friends. What a wonderful send-off. On our way back to the motel, we realized that our great adventure had finally begun.

The next morning dawned bright and sunny. We walked to a nearby restaurant and had breakfast before checking out of the motel. We were anxious to get started, but there was also the feeling of "Oh my God, what were we thinking?" We were facing months of pedaling, over mountains and across plains, before reaching our destination. At that point we were both a bit, or should I say a *lot*, overwhelmed.

It was time to look at this a little differently. We pulled out our map to see where we would be camping that evening. Aha, Detroit Lake campground was about fifty miles away. We could do that!

There was a lesson here. If you focus on a far destination, or a large goal, it can be overwhelming. But, if you break it down into small segments, it suddenly becomes very manageable. Just enjoy the journey, and the destination will take care of itself. We had to remind ourselves about this lesson a number of times along the way.

We got our first taste of hill climbing later that morning, as we began our climb into the Cascade Mountains. After about twenty-five miles, we stopped and had a bite to eat. We were only half way through the day, and we were already getting tired. By the time we got to our campground near Detroit Lake, we were more than ready to stop. We thought we were really in shape and ready for all this riding. What we had not considered was that, at the end of the day, there would be no TV to watch and no soft bed to climb into. We had to set up the tent and roll out the sleeping bags. Then, in the morning we had to pack it all up, get back on the bikes, and do it all over again.

While we were sleeping, it started to rain.

The next morning, we got our first real experience of breaking camp in the rain, and our bright yellow rain gear got its first real test. We rode to the town of Detroit, which was just a few miles away, and stopped for breakfast.

While we were eating, a big guy strolled over and stopped beside our table. As I looked up, he seemed to be about the size of Paul Bunyan. I'm only 5'-6" tall, and from my perspective, this guy looked huge. He looked down at us, and in a slow, lazy sort of way he said, "Hope you folks have *chains* for them strange-looking *bicycles* outside."

"Oh?" I asked. "Why would we need chains?"

"Because it's snowing up on the pass," he said. "Just came that way in my log truck, and there's already about two inches on the ground."

"Wow," I said, "thanks for the bad news."

He just grinned, tipped his cap, and walked out.

I looked over at Kris and said, "Now, what? That was where we had planned to stop tonight. After what we just heard, I don't think that's such a good idea."

"As usual," Kris said, "I have a plan. What would you think about catching a ride to the other side of the mountain?"

"You mean like sticking our thumbs out?" I asked. "Do you really think that's a good idea?"

"Since it's snowing up there, I don't think we have any other choice," she replied. "I know that wasn't part of the plan, but we might as well do it."

When we got back on the road, the rain was already getting a little slushy. So, we stuck out our thumbs, hoping that someone would feel sorry for us.

A number of cars passed us before a large pickup truck pulled over. As I ran up to the truck, an elderly man rolled down the window and asked, "Are you two really looking for a ride?"

"Yes sir," I answered. "We were told that it's snowing up on the pass, and as you can see, this rain is already starting to get a little thick. Would you be so kind as to give us a lift to the other side of the mountain?"

"Sure thing," he said. "Just put those things in the back and hop in."

So, we put our bikes in the back and climbed in.

"Thank you so much," I said. "I'm Jake, and this is my wife Kris."

"My name is Sam," he said, "and this is my grandson Billy. This is really a first for me," Sam said. "I travel this stretch a lot, but I have never been flagged down by a bike-rider before. Oh, I see plenty of them struggling up this mountain, but none of them has ever stuck out his thumb for a ride. So where you folks headed, over to Sisters or Bend?" he asked.

Kris spoke up and said "No, we are headed for Portland, Maine."

"Did you say Portland?" Sam asked. "Aren't you headed in the wrong direction?"

"No, no," Kris replied, "I said Portland, *Maine*, like on the east coast."

"Maine?" Sam asked. "Isn't that somewhere over on the other side of the country, by New York City?"

"You are absolutely right," I said.

"That's a long way to be riding those fancy bicycles you folks got," he replied. "I can't imagine going to Maine, even by car, when we live in such a beautiful place like Oregon. What in the world prompted you folks to do such a thing?"

We told him about my wild hair and he just shook his head. "I've done some wild things in my day," he said, "but never anything quite like what you kids are planning to do. I sincerely hope it turns out well for you."

Sam took us up over the pass, and started down the other side. Just as the truck driver had said, there was already a couple inches of snow on the ground.

Once we got to where it had stopped snowing, I turned to Sam and said, "We really appreciate your help in getting us over the pass. I don't know about Kris, but I'm feeling a little guilty about letting you to take us all the way down the mountain."

Kris chimed in, "I have to agree with Jake. We can't thank you enough, but I think we need to get back on the bikes."

"Well," Sam said, "if you must, you must. But I'd be more than willing to take you all the way down to the next town."

"We appreciate the offer," I said, "but the sun is shining brightly and it looks like a great day to continue our ride."

So he stopped, wished us well, and we continued on our way.

Going down the mountain was a whole lot easier than going up. We came to call coasting down hills and mountains the *Reward* for the effort it took to climb them. That particular day we had a great reward, and we were actually able to combine two days of riding into one.

Later that day, as I was following Kris along a nice flat stretch of road, I noticed that one of her rear tires looked a little low. So we pumped it back up, and continued on our way. About a mile further on, that same tire looked low again. In fact, it seemed to be sagging as I watched. Guess it was time to investigate. When I removed the tire, I discovered that there was a thorn in the tire that had punctured the tube. I removed the thorn, replaced the tube, and we were on our way again. We had done some practice on changing tires, so it was not too bad. As it turned out, that would be her only flat tire for the entire trip, and I had three flats along the way. Early that evening we pulled in to a campground and set up our tent and sleeping bags. After patching the punctured tube, we called it a day.

The next day turned into a drying out day. Some of our stuff was wet from the soaking rain that we had run into on the other side of the mountain. We spread it all out in the sun to dry, and stayed an extra day at the campground. Later that afternoon, another cyclist pulled in. Curiosity got the better of us, so we went over and introduced ourselves.

"Always glad to meet fellow cyclists." he said. "My name is Bill, and I'm from Pennsylvania. Where are you folks from?"

"We're from Portland," I said, "and we've only been on the road for a couple days. So what brings you to Oregon?"

"Well," he said, "during most of the year, I am an elementary school teacher. But, during the summer, my wife lets me take some excursions by myself, to unwind after school is out. I have been doing this for five years now, and have logged over 15,000 miles. My goal is to ride through all forty-eight states, and I'm getting very close. This trip will do it."

"Wow, that's quite a record. Doesn't your wife worry about you when you're gone?" I asked.

"Oh sure she does, but I call home every other day. That seems to satisfy them, as long as they know I'm safe."

"I noticed you said them." Kris said. "That sounds like there may be some kids?"

"There certainly are," he said, as a smile lit up his face. "We have two beautiful daughters, ages seven and four. I miss them when I'm on my trips, but we make up for it when I get home."

"So when did you start?" Kris asked.

"About a week ago I flew to Seattle to begin this year's tour, just before Mount St. Helens blew the second time. By the time I got to Portland, all that ash had totally trashed my chain and bearings. I was fortunate to find a shop that could replace them, but it did delay me for a few days."

"We know all about that" I said. "We were out riding when the mountain blew the second time. We had to do the same thing. While our bikes were being fixed we spent most of that week shoveling ash into garbage bags. What a mess."

When I looked at his bike, I noticed a rather unusual sign on the back that read, "Caution: Tobacco Chewer."

"Bill," I asked, "what is with that sign?"

"Oh that" he said. "I always ride with a pinch of tobacco between my cheek and gums, and occasionally I have to spit. Whenever I ride with someone, I ride at the back of the group."

"Right," I said, "that sure makes sense to me. It's been a pleasure to meet you, but we should probably get back to our camp. By the way, would you like to ride with us tomorrow?"

"It would be my pleasure," he said. "Since you know where I'm camped, why don't you just meet me here?"

"Sounds like a plan," I said.

The next morning, after breaking camp, we rode over to meet Bill.

When he saw us coming, his eyes opened wide and he said, "Wow, recumbents. I've read about these things, but I've never seen a real one. Could I try it before we leave?"

"Sure," I said.

He sat down and started pedaling, no wobbles, like he had been riding one for a long time. I yelled to him to take a ride around the campground. When he got back, he was laughing.

"Wow," he said, "this is really comfortable. I might have to look into these when I get back home."

That evening we rode into a small town in central Oregon. We stopped in at a local café for dinner, and asked the waitress if there was a campground anywhere close.

"I don't know of any campgrounds," she said, "but we have a small park in the middle of town where you could set up your tents. It has restroom facilities, and it seems like it might be the ideal spot."

When we got our tents set up in the small park, the sun was going down, and we decided to call it a day. We had been asleep for a couple of hours when we heard a commotion outside and the tent started to shake. I grabbed my tire pump and headed for the door. Outside, I saw Bill with a small baseball bat, and he was chasing some kids across the lawn. They jumped into a car, and the tires were smoking as they made their escape. I didn't think we would see them again.

When Bill returned, he was furious! I would not want him chasing *me*; he was about six feet tall, and quite muscular.

"I can't get away from those damn kids," he yelled, "even on my rides! That's why I do these rides, to get away and unwind. Now I even have to put up with them when I'm camping. And look at that, one of my tent poles is broken. It's a good thing I didn't catch those little …"

"Bill, Bill," I said as I ran over and grabbed his arm. "It's okay, they're gone, just settle down."

When he looked at me, I could see the fire in his eyes. "You don't have to put up with all their …"

"Bill," I said, "they're gone, and I seriously doubt if they're coming back."

With still a hint of that fire, he said, "If they know what's good for them, they won't."

When we got back to the tents, we saw that they had pulled up all the tent stakes, and indeed, one of Bill's tent poles was bent. He went to his bags, pulled out a roll of duct tape, and threw the bags back on the ground. I could tell that he was still fired-up.

"Never hurts to be prepared," he said through clenched teeth. "You never know when some *idiot* will try to ruin things for you."

With the help of the duct tape, we were able to fix his bent pole. All three of us were pretty wound up at that point, so we decided to stay up for a while. First thing on the agenda, put the tents back together. Ours just needed the stakes put back on the corners, but Bill's tent had collapsed. So, we helped him resurrect it, and then sat down to unwind a bit.

"Sorry about that outburst," Bill said. "If you will indulge me, I need to unwind. As I may have told you, I teach sixth-grade science. This incident reminds me of something that I ran into with my class. Whenever we do a project that takes a couple of days, I always find out that someone has been messing around while I'm not there. I don't know if it's one of the kids in my class, or an outsider, but it never fails."

"That has got to be frustrating," Kris said. "I'm just glad that I don't run into that kind of thing in my job. I work at a large hospital in Portland as a lab-tech, and someone messing with our lab work could affect someone's life."

"Oh, indeed it could," Bill said. "Well, let's see. I found out that Kris works as a lab-tech, but what do you do, Jake?"

"I was a designer at a manufacturing plant. We designed the machines that actually did the cutting and shaping of the parts that we manufactured."

"And what did they manufacture?" Bill asked.

"They manufactured the long bars, and chains, for chain saws."

"Now wait," he said, "you said, *I was*. Does that mean you *don't* anymore?"

"Very astute," I replied. "That is exactly what it means. Kris and I both quit our jobs to do this trip."

"Wow," Bill said, "so, tell me about this trip of yours."

"Would you believe that we're headed for Portland, Maine?" Kris said.

"Maine?" he asked. "You did say Maine? Oh, there has got to be a story behind this. Tell me more."

We told him all about my wild hair, and how we got the bikes. After that, we were all starting to get sleepy again, so we crawled back into our tents for a few more hours of shuteye.

The next morning we flagged down a police car.

"Good morning, officer," I said. "We camped here in the park last night, and about midnight a group of kids descended on us. They pulled up all the tent stakes for both our tents and ran."

"I chased after them," Bill said, "but they jumped into a dark Mustang convertible and took off. Fortunately they didn't steal anything, and only one of my tent poles got bent. We were able to fix it, but we were pretty shook up.

The police officer nodded his head, and said "I know who the car belongs to. It's the only one in town. Do you want to press charges?"

"No," I replied, "we just thought you should know about it."

"So here is the situation," he explained. "School is out for the summer, and it was a Friday night in a small town. With not much to do, some of the young people tend to go out and create their own entertainment."

"Unfortunately, that turned out to be us," Bill said.

"Unfortunately," the police officer replied. "I will get in touch with the young man driving the convertible, and perhaps shake him up a bit. Those kids shouldn't be harassing people like you. Sorry you had to go through that."

We thanked the police officer, and went to have breakfast at the same café where we had dinner the night before.

Before we went inside, Bill turned to us and said, "I am really glad that we were together last night, to fend off those kids. I would really like to set a little faster pace, so I'm going to head on alone. I truly enjoyed our time together, and I hope your trip to Maine goes well."

So we said our good-byes, and he went riding on down the road. It was the last we saw of him. Hope he made his goal of riding through all 48 states.

When it was just the two of us, we settled into a routine of swapping leads. I would lead for a couple of miles, and then Kris would lead for a couple of miles. By doing this, we were a lot less tired at the end of the day. However, there were times when Kris would get a burst of energy and rocket away from me. Eventually I would catch up when she stopped to look at the flowers, or whatever.

We suspected that it was the bananas that prompted those bursts. I had one every couple hours, and it didn't take long before I could feel the added energy. The banana industry's profits must have spiked while we were on our trip.

After what seemed like forever, we finally reached the city of Ontario on the Oregon-Idaho border. That was one state down and a bunch to go. Before crossing over into Idaho, we decided to celebrate by staying in a motel, with a nice soft bed and a *shower*!

Idaho

After we crossed the Snake River into Idaho, our first destination was Boise, the state capital. When we got there, we decided to stop by and see the Capitol Building. Since we could not find a safe place to park our bikes, we settled for just seeing the outside. It is a very impressive building that is modeled after the Capitol Building in Washington, DC.

When we continued on, we started hearing some clicking coming from Kris's rear wheels. Not a good sign, so we stopped at the first bike shop we came to. When we walked in with our bikes, a young man came over, gave our bikes a quick look, and said, "Recumbents, right? Wait right here, my boss has got to see this." He almost tripped over himself as he ran to the back room.

When his boss came out, he said, "Hi, my name is Rick, what can …?"

He had just spotted our bikes, and just stood there with his mouth open.

"Wow, recumbents," he said, "and one of them is a trike. I saw one those things advertised in a magazine, and they sure look interesting. Those seats look like they would be comfortable. Would you mind if I sat on one?"

"Sure," Kris said, "try mine."

As Rick sat down, I heard someone yell, "Hey guys, come on out here. Somebody just brought in a couple recumbents."

Pretty soon the whole staff had gathered around, checking out our bikes.

As Rick stood back up, he said, "I was right about that seat. Would you mind if the guys tried them out?"

I looked over at Kris and she nodded. "Sure," I said. "We did come in here for a different reason, but we can get to that in a few minutes."

One by one they all gently sat down and put their feet on the pedals. I could hear their discussion in the background.

One guy was saying, "I like that two-wheeler," and another said, "no way, man, the three-wheeler is the way to go. You don't have to worry about the balance."

Another guy said, "With seats that comfy, who cares about two-wheels or three-wheels. I'd take both."

Rick came over to me and asked, "How difficult is your two-wheeler to ride?"

"Not too bad," I replied, "but the balance is quite different. When you first start out, it feels like you're going to tip over. The first time I tried it, I was all over the street. But once you catch on, it's really a smooth ride."

As the guys continued to look over the bikes, I heard one say, "Good grief, check out that chain. What is it, about two full chains?"

"That's right," I said, "two full chains."

They all stood around for a few more minutes before Rick said, "Okay guys, time to get back to work." Then he turned to us, and asked, "Now, how can we help you?"

"We've been noticing that the spokes on the trike's rear wheels are clicking." I said. "Any idea what might cause that?"

"I know exactly what causes that," Rick said. "You have a couple loose spokes. We just have to find them and tighten them up. Give me a few minutes, and we'll have you on your way again."

He rolled it into the back room, and about fifteen minutes later brought it back out. "You had several spokes on each wheel that were loose. Got them all tight, and you're ready to go, no charge. It was a real treat to see those recumbents up close, and we all hope you have a safe trip."

It was late afternoon when we arrived at a campground on the outskirts of Boise. After setting up our tent, we noticed that there were two ladies, a blond and a red-head, camped next to us. We also noticed that they had Washington state license plates on their car. So, we walked over to introduce ourselves.

"Hi," Kris said, "I'm Kris, and this is my husband Jake. We're camped right over there, and we noticed your Washington license plates."

"Oh, hi," said the blond, "I'm Judy, and this is Sally. Are you from Washington too?"

"No, we're actually from Portland," Kris said.

"Are you serious?" Sally asked. "We saw you come cruising in on some odd looking bikes. Did you ride them from Portland?"

"Indeed we did," I answered. "They are called recumbent bicycles, kind of a new design."

"I'll say they are," Sally replied. "It looked like you were carrying all your gear on them, as if you are traveling somewhere."

"Maybe they're going to Salt Lake City, like we are," Judy said to Sally.

"Well, not quite," I said. "What's the attraction in Salt Lake City?"

"Well," Sally said, "we're Mormons from Seattle, and we both sing in a church choir there. We have never seen the Tabernacle Choir perform, so we're on our way there to see them. It's going to be an quite an exciting experience."

"Where are you folks headed?" Judy asked.

"Our destination is Portland, Maine," Kris answered.

"Did you say Maine?" Judy asked. "There must be a story here, am I right?"

"Yes, you are right," I said.

We told them all about my wild hair, and how we found out about our bikes.

While we were talking, we heard a rumble coming from the highway. We looked up and saw a group of Harley Davidson motorcycles pulling into the campground. Our campsite happened to be right across the road from the large group area, which is where all of those motorcycles wound up. There must have been about twenty of them, and the sound of all those Harleys in one spot was unbelievably loud. It was a relief when they all shut down.

"If you hear a loud scream in the middle of the night," Judy said, "come save us." We chuckled over that one, and watched as the dust cleared.

The group across the road paid us no heed as they set up their camp. Then they all disappeared into their tents for a while, and came out wearing shorts, t-shirts, and sweats instead of the black leather outfits they rode in with. One of the guys came walking by, with towel in hand, so I decided to walk with him to the restroom/shower building.

"Hi, my name's Jake," I said as we shook hands.

"Name's Dave," he replied.

"I've never seen so many Harleys in one place," I said. "Where are you folks from?"

"We all belong to a Harley club in L.A., and we're on our way to Yellowstone." he said.

"We heard you coming down the highway," I told him, "and when you wound up across the road from us, the two gals camped next to us were a little freaked. However, when you changed out of your leathers into normal clothes, they were quite relieved."

"We get that reaction a lot," Dave said. "Actually, we're just normal people with normal jobs who happen to ride Harley's. The outlaw gangs have really given the Harley a bad name. Wish there was some way to change that. So where you folks headed?"

"We're on our way to Portland, Maine," I replied.

"Are you traveling with those two ladies?" he asked.

"No," I said, "we just happened to strike up a conversation with them."

"Well," Dave said, "hope you have a safe trip."

A little later, one of the guys came over and said, "Hi, my name's Rusty. Would you folks like to join us for a beer? We've all been looking at those contraptions parked next to your tent, and we're dying of curiosity."

"Sure thing," I said, "we'll bring our bikes with us."

"Bikes," he asked, "as in bicycles? They're not going to believe this. Whenever you're ready, just come on over."

A few minutes later we walked our bikes across the road. They handed us a beer, and we proceeded to tell them about our weird contraptions, and how we got them. They all had a big laugh when I told them about my sore butt problem.

One of the ladies asked, "Are you really going to ride those things all the way to Maine?"

Almost in unison they all said, "WAY TOO MUCH WORK!"

Several of them wanted to sit on the bikes, and as one of the guys sat down on my bike, he said, "Hey, this is almost like a chopper, but it's missing an engine."

They wanted to know all about our trip, and how we came up with such a ridiculous idea. We told them about my wild hair, and some of our experiences, before we finally decided to call it a day.

The next morning, we were on our way bright and early, riding down Interstate 84. Idaho is one of the few states where the interstate is open to bicycles. We really enjoyed riding on that nice wide shoulder as the 18-wheelers roared by. We were a little concerned that the windblast might knock us over, but that was not the case. Instead, those big rigs created a vacuum that sucked us along, and gave us a free ride for a short way.

After about an hour on the road, we heard that familiar rumble, and those Harley riders motored on by. There was a sort of camaraderie between cyclists and motorcycle riders, and we always exchanged waves whenever we crossed paths.

Our next stop was a place called "Craters of the Moon." It is an ocean of lava flows, with scattered islands of cinder cones and sagebrush, at an elevation of almost 6,000 feet. We were very careful where we rode, since those cinders had points and edges sharp enough to puncture a bicycle tire. However, the roads were quite clean and we made it through with no mishaps.

It was a landscape much like what you might expect to see on the moon. The Apollo 14 astronauts actually visited Craters in 1969 in preparation for their trip to the moon.

That evening we stopped in a small town called Arco. (Say, isn't that the name of an oil company?) The next day, for a distance of 70 miles between Arco and Idaho Falls, the only cars we saw had an atomic energy logo on them. There was only one town in that stretch, about a half-mile off the main highway, and it was called Atomic City! Occasionally we would see concrete bunkers back off the main highway. They all had gravel roads leading to them, and a gate with a sign that read "Restricted: Government Vehicles Only." Once we got to Idaho Falls, we thought that maybe we should get checked for radiation!

The following day was very hot, and we had a short ride of about twelve miles to the base of the mountains that we had to cross. Kris's knees were not feeling too good, so we decided to stop and rest up for the next day's climb. That turned out to be our shortest day's ride of the trip. We spent the day reading, talking, napping, and just taking it easy.

The next morning, as we crawled out of our sleeping bags, the sun was already up. I could feel that there would be no relief from the heat. After packing our gear, I asked Kris how she was feeling.

"That day of rest was just what I needed," she said. "My knees feel great and I'm ready to go. Bring on the mountains."

That was music to my ears, because I thought the whole trip might be in jeopardy. As usual, Kris was up to the task, and we were about to experience a very typical day of riding in the mountains.

After stopping for a hearty breakfast, we were ready to tackle that climb. We started out easy to give our knees and legs a chance to get warmed up. After a few miles the grade started getting steeper. We were getting to that part of the climb where we would have to gear down, and just keep turning those pedals. As the terrain got steeper, and we rode slower, it seemed like we could have walked faster. I just kept telling myself that my goal was to make it to the next curve in the road.

As the day went on, I could feel the heat draining the energy out of my body, and the aching muscles in my legs. Again, the goal was just the next turn in the road. When the hot sun was finally at our backs, I knew that we could not be far from the top of the pass. Suddenly I heard Kris let out a yell of jubilation. She had spotted the summit! It seemed as though all my tired and aching muscles were rejuvenated with the sound of that yell. When we reached the top, we could see our *reward* for that long, hot, grueling climb. There were miles and miles of coasting downhill.

After an exhilarating ride down the other side of the mountain, we pulled into a small town. A restaurant was calling to us, so we decided to heed its call. We were definitely ready to stop and relax after our day's ride.

When we finished our dinner and walked outside, we noticed that there was a storm headed our way. Our destination was a campground at the edge of town, so we jumped on our bikes and headed that way. When we pulled in, the wind was already blowing pretty hard. The manager said he only had one site left, and that it was out in the open.

"With that storm coming in," I said to Kris, "I don't see that we have much choice."

"I don't usually offer this," he said, "but that storm looks kind of nasty. I have a full sized teepee set up around back, and you're welcome to use it."

We just looked at him and said, "A teepee? Like an Indian teepee?"

"That's right" he replied, "like an Indian teepee. It's big enough to accommodate both of your sleeping bags and your bikes"

"Honey," Kris said, "I really don't like the idea of trying to set up our tent in this wind. Let's take the teepee."

I had to agree with her, so we took it. On the way around back we almost got blown over. Surely a teepee couldn't stand up to that kind of wind, but there it was in all its glory. Once we got inside, we discovered that it was pretty big. There was a fire pit in the middle, which looked to have been used, and an open top.

"Honey," I exclaimed, "this thing has an open top! We're going to get soaked. I think I had better ask the manager how to close it."

But when I opened the flap to get out, the storm had already arrived, and it was pouring down rain. Hey, wait a minute, if it was already raining, why weren't we getting wet with that top open? Perhaps the Indians knew some things that we didn't.

Somehow, the poles that you see sticking out the top catch the rain and channel it to the ground outside. I still don't know how that works, but it sure did that night. We could hear the storm howling outside, but inside the teepee it was dry and calm. After we got things situated, we settled down to a great night's sleep.

The next morning dawned sunny and clear, and we were on our way again. We had a very good day, and it was late afternoon when we stopped in Ashton, Idaho for some pie and coffee. We asked the waitress how far it was to a particular campground that we had set as our destination for the day.

"It's about ten or twelve miles" she said, "but are you sure you want to ride your bikes up there this late in the day?"

I said "Sure, ten or twelve miles should be a breeze, about another hour. Why, is there some problem with the road?"

"Well, you'll have to ride up the Ashton Grade" she said, "It's a stretch of road about six miles long just north of town. The highway goes up to the Snake River Plain, and it's about an eight percent grade."

"Yikes," Kris said as she turned to me, "that's an awfully steep grade. Remember the Sunset Highway back home? That was six percent, and some of my friends would avoid it because it was too steep."

"Oh, come on," I replied. "Surely it can't be *that* bad. Besides, it's way too early to stop."

So we decided to tackle "The Ashton Grade." After all, it was only six miles. Were we in for a surprise! Have you ever tried to ride a bicycle up the side of your house? That's almost what it seemed like.

After the first mile we stopped and rested. We had been in our lowest gear, just spinning away, and it didn't seem like we were getting anywhere. After some water and a banana, it was time to be on our way again. We stopped and rested after every mile, had some water and a banana, and continued on. When we finally reached the top, we understood why the waitress had cautioned us. That thing was a monster! We limped on to the campground, set up our camp, and settled in for a well deserved rest.

The next day we reached the beautiful vista of Targhee Pass at 7072 feet. It was located on the Continental Divide along the border between Idaho and Montana.

"You know," I said to the lady at the Information Center, "the climb from our campground to the Divide was pretty easy."

She just grinned and said, "You folks probably came up the Ashton Grade. Everyone who comes up *The Grade* is disappointed when they reach the Divide. However, the fifteen mile ride down the other side, into the town of West Yellowstone, Montana, should be a real treat."

Yellowstone National Park

The town of West Yellowstone, Montana, the west entrance to Yellowstone National Park, is at an elevation of 6,666 feet. The elevation change for those fifteen miles from Targhee Pass was only about four hundred feet, so our *reward* was not quite as thrilling as we had expected.

Since we were going to be riding at about 7,000 feet elevation, we decided to rest up in a motel room before tackling the park. After getting settled at the motel, we checked in with the local park ranger's office to see if there was anything we should be aware of. He told us that we should stay a safe distance from the elk and buffalo. Even though they appeared to be docile, they were still wild animals. Every year, a few unlucky visitors were killed by buffaloes because they chose to ignore the rules. It was not the animal's fault, since this was their home and we were the ignorant intruders.

As we entered the park the next morning, we were greeted by a thick forest of tall spindly lodgepole pine trees that cover about 80 percent of the park. We felt quite humbled by the enormity of what lay ahead of us. Yellowstone covers an area of almost 3,500 square miles. It is actually bigger than the states of Rhode Island and Delaware combined.

We had ridden for about a half hour when we started seeing buffalo and elk in clearings along the Madison River. There were also a lot of cars stopping with people jumping out to take pictures. We saw a woman jump out and start running out into a field to get a closer shot of a buffalo. Fortunately, her husband chased her down before she got too far. She could very easily have been one of those unlucky visitors the ranger had told us about. We saw a lot of people getting closer to the animals than they should have.

About an hour later, we got to our first rest stop at Madison Junction. After ordering our usual pie and coffee, we told our waitress about some of the people getting too close to the animals.

"We hear about that almost every day," she said. "Unfortunately, we also hear about people being gored by the buffalo. I've actually seen it happen, and it's not a pretty sight. Buffalo are very quick for a big animal. Most people don't realize that a buffalo can move that fast. Just watch from a safe distance and you should be okay."

We thanked her for the advice and continued on our way. A short time later we saw what appeared to be smoke rising beyond the trees to our left. We thought that there might be a fire or something. As we stopped to watch, we noticed that it was steam and not smoke. What we were seeing was the eruption of a geyser. As we watched, the hot water and steam just kept getting higher and higher. It was indeed a spectacular sight.

Not long after seeing that eruption, we pulled in to our next rest stop at Norris Junction. It was just a chance to get off the bikes and stretch before going on our way. We stopped by the gift shop to see what they had, and we spotted something that had us chuckling to ourselves. They were selling small vials of Mount St. Helens ash! We could have made a small fortune with all of that stuff that we shoveled into trash bags back home.

Since we had a short day, we decided to see some of the features of the park. Sitting right next to the Mount St. Helens ash display was a brochure for a walking trail that started near the gift shop. The brochure suggested allowing some time for the two mile loop, as there was much to see. That was no problem, but what would we do with the bikes? We called the clerk over to see if he had any suggestions.

"We would really like to do the loop described in this brochure," I told him. "However, we have two fully loaded bicycles that would probably be in the way if we took them on the trail. Do you have any suggestions?"

"First of all," he said, "bikes are not allowed on the boardwalk. But we do have a locked enclosure behind the gift shop. It is actually for our garbage dumpster, but if you don't mind the smell, perhaps you could put them there. Only the people who work here have access, so I don't think it would be a problem. Give me a minute and I'll take you back. By the way, my name is Jack."

A few minutes later Jack was back with someone to take over for him. When we walked outside, there were several people standing around our bikes.

Jack just stopped and stared. "I thought you said you had bicycles," he said. "Those things don't look like any bicycles I've ever seen."

"They are indeed bicycles, just a different design," I said. "They're called recumbent bicycles, and they're really comfy." Several of the people standing around had the same questions. They asked if they could sit on one, so we let them try the trike. Nearly every one of them remarked about how comfortable it was. After everyone had their turn, I brought Jack over to try it out.

As he gingerly lowered himself onto the seat, a big grin lit up Jack's face.

"Wow" he said, "you weren't kidding, this feels great. I have a bike at home, but it's nowhere near as nice as this."

Jack stood back up, gave the bikes another once over, and then led us around back to the locked enclosure. "Your bikes will be secure here while you go for your stroll. I think you will enjoy the loop. I'm still amazed every time I take that walk, and I've been around it half a dozen times. Have fun."

The two major areas in the Norris Geyser Basin are the Back Basin and the Porcelain Basin. We chose the Porcelain Basin, the smaller of the two, which has nine small geysers. We followed a boardwalk for the two mile loop around the basin.

There were warning signs posted along the way telling visitors to stay on the boardwalk, as temperatures in the pools were at or near boiling. After we had walked a short way we saw steam rising from some of the pools. Several of the pools were bubbling as if getting ready to erupt.

As we watched, one of the pools started bubbling more vigorously until a small spout began erupting in the middle of the pool. That small eruption continued to get bigger until it was about fifteen feet high. It stayed that way for a short time and then began subsiding. Before long the eruption was gone and all that remained was a bubbling pool again. We had just been given a show of nature at her most outrageous. We were treated to that same show at several other pools during our two mile excursion around Porcelain Basin.

Some of the pools were a rich blue color, and others had more of a greenish tint. There are algae that live in some of those hot acidic pools, which give the water a greenish tint. The ground and rocks around most of the pools was milky colored from the mineral deposits in the water. At one of the pools, the area around it was an orange color from the iron oxide in the water. Since the area was highly acidic, it had a very noticeable smell of sulfur.

After completing our trek around the boardwalk, we went back to the gift shop and retrieved our bikes. We thanked Jack for his help and were once again on our way.

About an hour later we reached Canyon Junction, our final destination for the day. Its name comes from the nearby scenic grandeur of the one-thousand foot deep Grand Canyon of the Yellowstone. The Yellowstone River runs north through the canyon. The Canyon is four thousand feet wide at the rim, and meanders for twenty miles north to the Narrows near Tower Junction.

We went straight to the campground and got settled in. After dinner we rode south along the North Rim Drive to see the Canyon. At one of the observation points, Lookout Point, we were able to see a huge falls called the Lower Falls. Does that mean that there is an Upper Falls? Indeed there is. The Yellowstone River plummets over the Upper Falls, a height of 109 feet, and then about a half mile further on over the Lower Falls, a height of 308 feet. The Lower Falls is twice the height of Niagara, and it is quite a sight to behold. The Canyon itself is very colorful, with colors from egg white to salmon pink. The colors are a byproduct of iron oxidization in the rock.

When we finally got back to our campsite, we pulled out our map to check out the next day's ride. There was nothing too serious, just another pass to climb. You know, work your tails off going up and then relax and coast down the other side.

Before turning in for the night, we were looking through a park brochure and it mentioned something about occasional thunderstorms. That was the farthest thing from our minds as it had been a beautiful clear day. So we put the brochure aside and snuggled in for a good night's sleep.

We had been asleep for about an hour or so when we awoke to the sound of … thunder? It was quite a ways off, so not to worry. A little later we were awakened again as the sky lit up, and shortly thereafter we heard more thunder. This time it seemed a lot closer, and it had started to rain. In what seemed like only a few minutes, the sky lit up again, just as the thunder crashed right over our heads! It was then that I noticed the aluminum poles that held up our tent. We were lying under half a dozen lightning rods! Just then I heard something go CA-RACK right close to our tent. I was out of that tent in a hurry to see what had happened. Some other campers were also out in the rain with flashlights. They were looking at a large tree not far away that had been hit by the lightning, and one of the branches was about ready to fall off.

It wasn't close enough to be of any danger, so we all crawled back into our tents as the storm moved away and the rain gradually stopped.

The next morning, we thought about how we really could have used a little more sleep. We were about to ride over the highest pass of the trip so far. Dunraven Pass, at 8,859 feet, lay ahead of us on our last day in the park. The pass is on the west flank of Mt Washburn, which is 10,243 feet. As we struggled up to the summit of Dunraven Pass, I was grumbling about how that stupid storm had kept us awake the night before. But we made it and were only too happy to get our *reward* on the other side, a nice long downhill coast. We were headed for Tower Junction, and then on out the northeast entrance.

As we were heading down the other side of the mountain, I saw a deer bounding down the embankment. Kris was quite a ways ahead of me and had no idea what was going on behind her. I could see the deer was going to cross the road right in front of me. At least I was hoping he would! With my brakes smoking and tires squealing he passed in front of me by about ten feet. Way too close for me!

As we approached Tower Junction, we could see towering cliffs off to the east. When we stopped for our usual pie and coffee we asked about the cliffs. They are called Specimen Ridge, where you can see over 100 different species of fossilized trees. While we were indulging, I told Kris about my close encounter with the deer. As I was telling the story my hands started shaking. It finally dawned on me how close I had come to disaster.

After our short stop we were once again on our way to Yellowstone's northeast exit. As we rode along the towering cliffs, we settled into our routine of swapping leads. I would lead for a mile or so, and then I'd drop back and tuck in behind Kris, while she led for a while.

We were both thinking about the wonders that we had seen in Yellowstone when we came upon a wide expanse of grassland called Lamar Valley. There we were treated to a large herd of buffalo who were feeding on the luscious grass in the valley. On the other side of the road was a herd of elk doing likewise. Once again we saw people getting way too close to the animals.

In the distance, on both sides of the road, we began noticing mountain peaks. After all, we were still in the Rocky Mountains area. To our left was Druid Peak, 9,583 feet high, and to our right was The Thunderer at 10,554 feet. In the distance we could see Barronette Peak soaring to 10, 404 ft. However, the highest pass of our trip still lay ahead of us.

Before long we reached the northeast exit of Yellowstone. During our time in the park we had seen some spectacular sights and nature at its most outrageous.

Montana

After leaving Yellowstone, our first stop was at Cook City, a small town just four miles outside the park. We took an extra day of rest there, so that we would be fresh when we took on Beartooth Pass.

Rising to nearly 11,000 feet, it was the highest elevation of any pass we would cross on the trip. We would have to ride sixty-three miles to reach the summit, so we were prepared for a tough day. However, the first thirty miles were a very gentle grade, and we were thinking that this might not be so bad after all. But, we had noticed some areas where there was snow alongside the road.

We stopped at a small combination store, motel, and gas station called "Top of the World Settlement" to get something to eat. The lady at the counter rang us up and said, "You folks are lucky you didn't come through here last week. We had temperatures in the teens and about three inches of snow. It's about sixty today, so it's warmed up quite a bit since then and the roads are clear now. Where are you folks headed?"

"We're headed for Red Lodge," I said.

"Then you'll be heading up over Beartooth?" she asked. "It sure is beautiful up there. By the way, where are you folks from?"

"We're from Portland, Oregon," Kris told her. "We're on a bicycle trip to Portland, Maine."

"You're on bicycles?" she asked. "You mean to tell me you rode bicycles all this way? That sure explains why you're dressed in t-shirts and shorts. I hope you have something warmer, because you'll need it up on Beartooth. It's always cold and windy up there."

After thanking her for the advice, we retrieved our jackets and changed into our polypropylene undershirts and wool long johns before we took off again.

A few more miles up the road it started to get decidedly steeper. Had it gone straight up the mountain, we probably would have seen grades of ten to fifteen percent. However, the road builders had built in quite a few switchbacks that cut down the grade.

When we finally reached the summit, actually a plateau at the top of the pass, there was a sign that read "Summit, Beartooth Pass; Elevation 10,974 Ft." There was also an arrow pointing up to the top of the mountain, a pointed rock formation that looked like a bear's tooth.

The lady at the store was absolutely right. It was quite chilly up there, and the wind never let up. As we rode around up there, we would have the wind in our face, then the road would turn and the wind would be at our back, and so on.

It suddenly dawned on us that we had already ridden sixty three miles, and we still had to get down off that rock! With our hands already cold and cramped, how were we going to do that? Would we have to swallow our pride and look for a ride, again? Neither of us could come up with a better solution. So we stuck out our thumbs, looking for some help.

There were quite a few vehicles that passed us by, before a small pickup pulled over. We explained our predicament to the driver, and he said he would be glad to help. However, he had his two sons with him so we would have to sit in the back with our bikes. Not a problem. As we started to head down the other side, we noticed how slow he was going. The road was steep, and there were switchbacks that continued all the way down the face of the mountain. Had we tried to ride down, we both would have been in serious trouble within a mile or so.

When we reached the bottom, the man stopped and said he would have to let us out. We thanked him profusely, and we went our separate ways. It didn't take long to get to Red Lodge, where we spotted a tavern that was advertising pizza. We hadn't had pizza since we left Portland, so we decided to sample their cooking.

We were just getting started on our first piece, with a beer to wash it down, when a man walked over to our booth.

"Do you folks belong to those odd-looking bikes outside?" he asked.

"Indeed we do," I replied.

"I saw you out on the road earlier," he said. "I thought to myself that those were some strange looking contraptions. When I came back here for a beer, there they were again. Would you mind if I joined you for a few minutes?"

"Sure," I said, "have a seat. Hope you don't mind if we finish our pizza. We've been riding most of the day and we're pretty hungry. By the way, I'm Jake and this is my wife, Kris."

"Name's Joe," he said as we shook hands. "So tell me, what do you call those things you're riding? I've never seen anything like them."

"They're called recumbent bicycles," I replied. "A mechanic back home designed and built them for us. They're really comfy and fun to ride."

"I looked them over as I was coming in," he said, "and they sure are different. One of them has three wheels, what's with that?

"Oh, that's mine," Kris said. "I can't ride Jake's without falling over, so the builder put two wheels in back to make it stable."

"Makes sense to me," Joe said. "You said back home" he inquired. "Just where might that be?"

Kris chimed in with "That would be Portland, Oregon."

Joe's mouth dropped open and he sort of stuttered "You rode those things all this way? Whatever possessed you to do such a thing?"

"Well," Kris said, "a little over a year ago, Jake came up with this weird idea about riding our bikes across the country. He called it his wild hair."

"Whoa," Joe exclaimed. "I've heard of some strange ideas, but that one takes the cake!"

Kris smiled and said, "That's pretty much what I said. I thought he had lost his mind. But he can be very persuasive, and so here we are, on our way to Portland, Maine."

Joe's eyebrows raised as he said, "Now wait a minute. Did you say Portland, Maine? Is that for real?" As we nodded he continued, "But, isn't that way over there on the east coast?"

"That's right," I said. "We still have a long way to go, but, it's been quite an experience so far."

When we finally finished our pizza, Joe asked, "Where are you folks planning to stay tonight?"

As I was taking my last sip of beer, Kris said, "We were planning to stay at a campground a few miles down the road."

"Hmm, doesn't sound very inviting to me," Joe said. "Tell you what. I have a cabin on the edge of town, and my wife and daughter went up to Billings for a few days. Would you consider spending the night there? I have plenty of room, and you could sleep in a real bed instead of those sleeping bags."

We were a little leery about spending the night with a stranger, but we liked the idea of sleeping in a real bed. Joe noticed our hesitation and called another guy over to our table.

"Andy," Joe said, "I asked these folks if they would like to spend the night at my cabin, but they seem a little leery."

"Well, I can certainly understand why." Andy had a very serious look on his face as he turned to us. "Nobody in their right mind would spend the night with this guy."

When Andy looked back at Joe, they both doubled over with laughter.

When the laughter subsided Andy said, "Sorry folks, just a little joke there. You could probably not meet a more upstanding guy than Joe. He and I have been friends for years, and I can sincerely vouch for him. By the way, you two are in for a treat."

I guess we would find out what that meant. We put our bikes in the back of Joe's pickup, and he drove us out to a huge two story log home near the edge of town.

When we got out of the truck, Kris just stood there with her mouth open.

"Uh… Joe?" I stammered. "Didn't I hear you say cabin?"

He chuckled and said, "My wife and I laughingly refer to this as our cabin, because it's made of logs. She came into quite a large inheritance when her folks passed away, so we decided to use it to build a nice home. We designed it ourselves, with the features we wanted in a home, and then had someone build it for us. It took about a year to complete, but it was worth the wait."

When we walked in the door, Kris and I just stood there staring. There was an open beamed ceiling, and a large staircase that led up to a wood railing on the second floor loft. In the middle of the house was a huge rock fireplace that went all the way to the ceiling.

"Come on," Joe said, "let me show you around."

On the other side of the fireplace was a kitchen that would make a gourmet chef drool. It had a commercial-sized refrigerator/freezer and gas range, and the counters and island were covered with polished concrete. Along one wall, beneath a window that looked out on the mountains, was a large, copper farmer sink.

The rest of the place looked like something that you would see in magazines.

"Joe," I exclaimed, "this place is magnificent."

"Thanks," he said, "it has been like a dream come true for us. We still pinch ourselves sometimes, to make sure that this is all real. We just love it."

After the tour, we settled down in front of that massive fireplace. When you have a full tummy, and a nice warm place to relax, what usually happens? Yup, after a few minutes I nodded right off.

Joe took the hint and took us up to his daughter's room on the second floor. It had a nice queen-sized bed and a private bath with a shower. I think we must have almost run him out of hot water. The next morning he fixed us a great breakfast, and took us back to the highway so we could continue our trip. Kris and I still talk about Joe's *cabin*.

A few days later we entered the Crow Indian Reservation, and stopped at the Information Center. We were on our way to the Little Bighorn Battlefield where the Lakota Sioux and Cheyenne Indians annihilated George Armstrong Custer and his troops. At the information center we were told that it would be alright for us to stop at the battlefield. But, since we were on bicycles, we probably should not stop at any of the towns inside the reservations. That sounded kind of ominous, so we decided to heed the warning.

The battlefield had an eerie feel to it, as if the spirits of the dead were still there. We walked our bikes around on the paths provided to get a sense of what took place there. Custer and his men never had a chance. They were armed with single-shot Springfield rifles, but the Indians had a varied assortment of repeating rifles. The Indians simply outnumbered and outfought Custer's troops. After all, the Indians were fighting in their own back yard, and knew all the ways to use the rugged terrain to sneak up on the troops. If you are any kind of history buff, I highly recommend going there.

Then it was back on the road through the rest of the Crow Reservation and the Northern Cheyenne Reservation. The only stops we made were at restaurants, to use the restrooms, and be on our way again. We rode about seventy miles that day before we reached Ashland, just beyond the Cheyenne reservation. It had been a very long, tiring day, so we stayed at a motel and got a good night's rest.

The next day we took our time and stopped whenever and wherever we wanted to. Forty-five miles later, we finally wound up in a small town called Broadus. The following day we encountered another steep grade, similar to the Ashton Grade. Only this one was a lot longer, and not quite so steep.

Oh, did I mention that this one was *downhill?* Yes, indeed, we were able to get our reward for that long day of riding through the reservations. The road was smooth with long, sweeping curves, so we just let the bikes run. At one point I looked at my computer, and it was reading fifty miles-per-hour. Woo-hoo! That was a real blast.

After a while the grade ran out, and we coasted down to a reasonable riding speed. We were riding southeast when we came upon a sign that read "Welcome to Wyoming." What? We thought we were headed for South Dakota, the home of Mount Rushmore and the Badlands. What's this about Wyoming? We stopped and consulted our map, and sure enough, the road we were on just clipped the northeast corner of Wyoming.

South Dakota

As we were riding through Wyoming, we could see a town in the distance, which turned out to be Belle Fourche, South Dakota. By the time we actually got there, it had been a long day, so we stopped at the first motel we came to.

The lady at the desk smiled and said, "We have one room left for tonight, and it is probably the last one in town. There is a professional rodeo taking place here tomorrow, and all the motels are full."

"That sounds like it might be fun," I said. "Do you have a room available for tomorrow night?"

"I'm afraid not," she said. "We are completely booked for tomorrow night."

We thanked her and went to our room. After cleaning up, we went riding around town. There were people everywhere! A parade was about to take place, so we ducked into a fire station to get out of the way. They had their big doors open, and they gave us a warm welcome.

After we introduced ourselves, they wanted to know all about our odd-looking bikes. We gave them the whole story about the bikes and how comfy they were to ride. Of course, they all had to sit on them to see just how comfy they were.

One of the firemen asked, "Did you come here for the rodeo?"

"Well," I said, "not exactly. We are actually on a cross country trip. We started in Portland, Oregon about a month ago, and we're on our way to Portland, Maine."

"Are you serious?" one of them asked. "How far is that, about two thousand miles? That's a long trip in a car, but on a bicycle? Sounds like *way* too much work."

"So, where are you staying?" another one asked.

Kris told them, "We got lucky and snagged the last available room in town for tonight, but they're booked up for tomorrow night. We were considering going to the rodeo tomorrow, as neither one of us has ever been to one. But we might have to skip it, because we have no safe place to put the bikes."

One of the firemen spoke up, "Hey, why don't you just stop by here tomorrow and we'll keep an eye on your bikes. That way you won't have to miss the rodeo. I've been to a couple, and they are really exciting."

What a wonderful gesture by the firemen.

They asked where we would be heading next, we told them we would be heading east after the rodeo.

"That is probably *not* such a good idea," one of the firemen said. "The road east goes right through the Standing Rock Indian Reservation, and there have been some *incidents* there recently. You might want to consider going south to Spearfish, and bypass the reservation."

We thanked them for the advice, and headed back to the motel. The next day was bright and clear, the perfect Fourth of July. We checked out of the motel and headed for the fire station. They were glad to see us again, and told us that they would take care of our bikes, and to have a great day.

The rodeo started about noon. The bulls were big and tough, and quite a few cowboys wound up in the dirt. It's a good thing that the clowns were out there to distract the bulls, or some of those bull riders would have been in serious trouble. The broncos were bucking hard, but most of the riders stayed in the saddle. I was also very impressed with the riding ability of the women who competed in the barrel races. It was all well worth the price of admission, and we had a great time.

After an early dinner we went to collect our trusty steeds (that's rodeo talk), so we could be on our way. One of the firemen gave us directions to a campground just outside of Spearfish, and they all wished us well. As we headed down the road, we noticed that there was almost no paved shoulder. We tried to ride right on the white line, but even then cars were honking as they went by. Quite a few were yelling "get those things off the road." We had a number of very close calls, as the cars were not giving us any extra room.

When we arrived at the campground, we breathed a huge sigh of relief to be off that road. Both of us had a serious case of the shakes. That was the first time we had been involved in such a scary scenario. Was it going to be more of the same tomorrow? We would just have to wait and see.

The next day was a fifty-mile ride to Rapid City, but we were on a different road with a real shoulder to ride on. Perhaps the day before had just been folks letting off steam after the rodeo. But no, we encountered the same behavior. They were still honking and giving us a one-finger salute as they went by.

Rapid City was a bigger town with a few more amenities. We really were not up to camping so we found a motel again. In the room was a brochure for Mount Rushmore and a car rental agency. We both let out a yell of "Yea, let's do it!" We went back to the office to rent the room for an extra night, and to find out about the car rental agency. As it turned out, the car rental place was just down the street from the motel.

The next morning we walked to the car rental place, and in no time at all, we *drove* back to the motel. With a map and brochure in hand, we were on our way. It took us a little time to figure out how to get to Mt Rushmore, but we finally made it.

What an awesome spectacle. The heads of the four Presidents are incredibly large, and the likeness of each one is right on. It boggles the mind to think about how it was done. Each of those faces is sixty feet high. A crew of men worked on it for fourteen years at a cost of $900,000. When Gutzon Borglund, the primary sculptor, died in 1941, the project ended. No carving has been done since then, and none is planned for the future.

On the way to Rapid City on our bikes, we had bypassed a couple of places that we wanted to see. Since we were out and about, *with a car*, why not stop by Deadwood. A true old west town, it was founded following the discovery of gold in 1876. Its cemetery contains the graves of Wild Bill Hickock (who was killed in Deadwood while playing poker) and Calamity Jane. Many of the original buildings have been restored, and it was like stepping back in time. I almost expected to see a cowboy come walking down the street with a gun strapped to his hip, and spurs on his boots.

On our way back to Rapid City we drove past the town of Sturgis, the Mecca of Harley Davidson motorcycle riders. I've often wondered why the Harley riders chose that particular town for their annual roundup. Guess I should have asked those Harley riders at the campground in Boise. Oh well, time to return the car and get ready for a long day of *bicycle* riding through the Badlands.

The next day, as the road dropped us down into the Badlands, we beheld formations and grasslands that are hard to describe. The wind and rain have combined to sculpt the sandstone into a landscape that is almost surreal. Although the outrageous formations are beautiful, the large expanses of lush, tall grasslands are equally as beautiful. All the way through we marveled at its grandeur. It is another example of nature being outrageous, as were the mud pots and geysers in Yellowstone.

A few days later, we stopped in a small town to replenish our water supply. It was very hot, and we had both been going through a lot of water. We were told there was a fountain in the park where we could fill our bottles. So we proceeded to do so, since we still had about thirty-five miles before we got to Pierre, the capital of South Dakota. Then I took a sip from my bottle and almost choked. That water was so full of iron that it should have clanked when it hit the ground. It was *awful*!

There was a restaurant just down the street, so we stopped there and got our bottles refilled. We asked the waitress what the temperature was, and she told us it was 98 degrees! No wonder we were going through a lot of water. About a mile down the road I took another sip of water, and again, I almost choked. The water from the restaurant had a lot of iron in it too, but nowhere near as bad as the fountain in the park. Well, we would just have to make do, as there was nothing else until we got to Pierre.

The terrain on the way to Pierre was rolling hills. We would coast down one hill and ride up the next one. About five miles before we got to Pierre, we both ran out of water. No problem you say? We had been drinking like fools all day long, the temperature was 98 degrees, and now there was no more water. Within the next couple of miles, Kris started acting rather odd. She was coasting on the down side of the rolling hills and walking her trike up the hills. She was making no attempt to ride up the hills. When I stopped to walk with her, she told me to get away, that she did not need my help! However, I walked with her anyway. She didn't say anything else to me, she would just glare. This continued all the way to Pierre.

Finally, as we topped a rise, we saw Pierre below us. We jumped on our bikes and rode down into a blast furnace. At least that's what it felt like. We stopped at the first restaurant we came to, and we each proceeded to drink about a gallon of water. We asked the waiter what the temp was, and he said it was 105 degrees! Once Kris had some water in her system, she returned to her old self again. We found out later that we were both suffering from hypothermia. The lack of water affected me differently. About a mile before reaching Pierre I noticed that I was not sweating any more. I just thought, "Hey, alright. At least I didn't have to put up with that anymore." It should have been a warning sign, but neither of us realized what bad shape we were in.

Since we were in the capital city of South Dakota, we stayed at a motel and took an extra day to go see the Capitol. The State Capitol building houses the State Supreme Court on the second floor, and the Senate and House of Representatives on the third floor. The Senate Chamber accommodates one person from each of the thirty-five legislative districts. The House of Representatives is composed of two representatives from each district, for a total of seventy members.

While playing tourist in the sweltering heat outdoors, and the frigid cool of our air-conditioned room, we both developed colds. I guess we must have sweated the colds out of our systems, because we were back to normal when we crossed into North Dakota.

North Dakota

We were on our way to visit some friends we had not seen in some time. When we reached the town where they had their farm, we stopped at a small restaurant for our usual mid-afternoon snack of pie and coffee. As we were getting ready to leave, a man walked up to our table.

"Hi, my name is Ben," he said, "and I'm a reporter for the local newspaper. I was wondering if I could talk to you for a few minutes. Someone saw your bikes sitting outside of the restaurant and gave us a call. They said that they had never seen bicycles like that before. With all the gear you folks have on them, the caller suggested that there might be an interesting story."

Kris said, "Sure, why not. We're almost to our destination for the day, so we have some time to spare." We introduced ourselves and sat back down.

"And where might your destination be?" Sam asked.

"We have some friends that live on a farm just north of town" I said. "Their names are Fred and Nancy. When Fred's father died, they moved here to take over the farm. They were our neighbors in Portland."

"Sure," Ben said, "I know Fred and Nancy. They're really nice people. But you said you were their neighbors in Portland? Do you mean to tell me that you rode those contraptions all the way from Portland?"

"That's right," I said. I took a moment to look around, and noticed that we had the attention of most of the people in the small restaurant. I guess we were the oddity for the day. "Ben" I said, "it sure looks like a lot of these folks would be interested in what we have to say. Why don't we sit at the counter, so everyone can hear us?"

"Excellent idea," he said.

We walked over and sat at the counter, and Ben told everyone to gather around.

When everyone was settled, Ben raised his hand. "These folks are friends of Fred and Nancy, who live on a farm just north of town. They rode those strange looking bicycles out front all the way from Portland, Oregon. I'll just shut up now and let them talk."

"Hi folks" I said. "I'm Jake and this is my wife, Kris. A little over a year ago, I came up with an idea to ride our bicycles across the country.

69

Kris thought that I had been out in the sun too long, because that idea was just crazy!" They all chuckled at that, and I went on. "But, I persisted and she finally came around. As Ben mentioned, we started in Portland, Oregon, and our final destination is Portland, Maine. It's really been interesting so far. We've seen some amazing places, and met some wonderful people."

"I think I agree with your wife" one of the men said. "How did you come up with such an idea?"

"Would you believe a magazine article?" I replied. "I saw a story about a large group of people who rode their bikes from Virginia to Oregon. The idea just grabbed me and I couldn't shake it. So, I mentioned it to Kris, and here we are."

I noticed that one guy got up and looked out the window at our bikes. "So, what's with those weird bikes?" he asked. "Never saw anything like them before."

"I'm sure you've all seen those little narrow seats on a regular bicycle. In fact, a lot of you have probably sat on them. They're not very comfy, are they?" There was a murmur of agreement, so I continued on. "I didn't particularly like them either. They made my groin go numb. So, we confronted our local bike shop with my predicament. They told us about a bicycle builder who was building something called a recumbent bicycle. It's built lower than a standard bike and it has a chair like seat with a back rest, very comfortable. So we tried them out and decided that's what we wanted."

The fellow by the window said, "One of them has three wheels, what about that?"

"That would be mine," said Kris. "I could not ride Jake's bike without falling over, so the builder made one with three wheels. I don't have to worry about balance, and it suits me just fine."

"Sounds like my kind of bike" replied one of the women.

Kris looked at her and said, "Why don't we go try it out when we're done here."

Most of the men raised their hands and said "Me too."

That pretty much ended the questions, so we went outside to see the bikes. There were about a dozen people, and they all wanted to sit on the bikes. After obliging them, one of the guys had another question.

"Why don't they make more of these things, since they're so comfortable?" he asked.

"It has to do with bike racing" I told him. "Recumbents have been around for quite some time. In the 1930's, the International Racing Federation banned them because they were faster than a standard bike. Since that time, tinkerers were the only ones who made them, because of that ban."

That pretty much seemed to satisfy their curiosity, and they all finally left or went back inside. Ben had a few more questions, like how far we rode each day, where we had been so far, and whether we camped every night. After we answered his questions, he took a few pictures and thanked us for our time.

That whole incident was kind of a fluke. Our original intention was to have a quick snack, and continue on out to the farm to visit Fred and Nancy. When we finally got to their place, they asked if we would like to stay for a day or two. We said sure, it would be our pleasure. That gave me some time to do some tune-up work on the bikes. Both bikes needed new rear tires, and just general stuff that needed looking after.

The next day, Kris and I were catching up on things with Fred when Nancy came running in waving a newspaper and screaming, "Freddie! Freddie! Take a look at this!"

She had just been to the store, and had seen something amazing on the front page of the local newspaper. Our picture! Yes indeed, our story had made the front page. As a matter of fact, I still have that article.

After leaving Fred and Nancy's place, we headed northeast and wound up at a campground in Fargo. Now, is that in North Dakota or Minnesota? Actually, the Red River runs right through the middle of the town. In North Dakota it's called Fargo, and when you cross the bridge into Minnesota, it's called Moorhead.

Minnesota

The next morning we crossed that bridge into Minnesota, did our usual high five, and continued on our way. That evening we stopped at a campground, the first of four stops we had planned to make in Minnesota. When we packed up our tent the next morning, we had no idea that one of our stops was about to get bypassed.

About lunch time, we stopped at a small café. When the waitress came over, she said, "Hi, my name is Jill, and I'll be your server today." She noticed our helmets and asked, "Out for a short ride?"

We sort of chuckled, and Kris said, "Actually, we're out for a very long ride."

"So, how far is this very long ride?" Jill asked.

Kris was still smiling as she answered, "We'll explain when you bring our lunch."

A short time later, she returned with a tray full of food.

"Now," she said as she sat down, "what is this about a long ride? Are you guys going to Minneapolis or something?"

"I hope you don't mind if we eat while we talk," I said.

"Not a bit," Jill replied. "That's what you're here for."

"We are indeed going to Minneapolis," I said. "My brother lives there, so we're going to stop and see him. We're actually from Portland, Oregon, and …"

"What?" she exclaimed. "You're joking, right? You didn't really ride your bikes from Portland, Oregon, did you?"

"No joke," I said. "We did exactly that."

The surprised look on her face was priceless. "But," she stammered, "that's … that's … that's a very long way from here. How did you do that?"

I laughed and said, "Practice, practice, practice."

She laughed as she popped me on the shoulder.

"Just kidding" I said. "Actually, this trip has been in the works for well over a year. About two months ago, when the lease on our apartment expired, we threw the keys on the counter, locked the door behind us, and took off."

Jill looked a little confused. "So, do you have someone following you in a van?"

"Nope," Kris replied. "It's just the two of us. We have all of our gear stuffed in bags, and strapped on our bikes."

"But isn't that kind of scary?" Jill asked. "I mean, just the two of you, out there by yourselves?"

"You know," I said, "that's something we never even thought about. I guess we just figured that we would be okay."

"Wow," she said, "it's sure something *I* would think about. So, you're going to Minneapolis to see your brother. Are you heading back home after that?"

"Not quite," Kris said. "From there we're heading to Portland, Maine."

"Portland, Maine?" Jill asked, as if it were on some other planet. "Hmm, that's really interesting. You're riding *from* Portland *to* Portland. So, how long do you think it will take?"

"We figure we should be able to get there by the end of August," Kris answered.

"You know," she said, "sometimes I think about getting away for a while, like you guys are doing. But, right now, I have my little boy to take care of, which takes up most of my spare time. He's three years old and quite a handful, but I love that little rascal to pieces. Maybe when he's older, we can take a little trip of our own. But, until then, I've got to get back to work. I just loved hearing about your trip, and I will remember you guys for a long time." When she got up, she hesitated for a moment, and then turned back to us.

"By the way, your lunch is on me, and I hope you have a wonderful trip." As she walked away, I noticed a tear sliding down her cheek. She was one of the many wonderful people we met along the way.

After we left Jill, we went rolling merrily along. The roads were smooth, we had good weather, and "the force was with us." When we got to the place where we had planned to stop for the day, it was still early in the afternoon, so we decided to keep going until we got tired.

About dusk, we pulled into a small town and decided to call it quits for the day. When I checked my computer, it showed that we had ridden *one hundred and ten* miles. I thought that it must be a mistake, but when I checked Kris's computer, it had the same mileage! Wow, we had just completed what cyclists call a century, riding one hundred miles in a day. To celebrate, we checked into a motel, cleaned up, and went to a nice restaurant to toast the day.

The next day we rode to Minneapolis. My brother Bob and his wife, Lisa, lived there. I had contacted him when we were planning the trip, to see if we could stop by. He told me that we had better, since we had not seen each other for quite a while. When we reached the outskirts of the city, we called Bob and told him where we were. A little later he pulled up in a big van, jumped out, and gave me a big hug. After I introduced him to Kris, we piled our bikes into the van, and he took us back to his home, a two-story house on a cul-de-sac. After hugs and introductions, we had to give them an explanation about the *weird bikes* that we were riding.

As we were walking in, I said to Bob, "Wow, this is a nice place. Did you win the lottery or something?"

"No," Bob chuckled, "no jackpot. After living in an apartment for a few years, we decided that we wanted something nice. So, when this house came on the market, we jumped on it."

Lisa grabbed Kris and said, "You've got to see this. I like to cook, so we were looking for something that had a nice kitchen. When I walked in here, I just knew this was it."

The kitchen looked to be about as big as the living room. It had an island, lots of counter space, and really nice appliances. It seemed ideal for someone who likes to cook.

After showing us around, Lisa took us upstairs to our room. We cleaned up, and met them back in the living room.

"I am just curious about something," I said. "Here it is, the middle of the week, and you two are home in the middle of the afternoon. How does that work?"

Lisa replied, "When you called Bob and told him when you were going to be here, we both put in for some vacation. We wanted to be here for you. After all, you came a long way to see us."

"We really appreciate that," I said. "Now, what do you guys do to afford a place like this?"

"Well," Bob explained, "I'm a foreman at a manufacturing plant, and I got transferred here from a subsidiary plant in Wisconsin. Lisa was fortunate enough to land a position as a private secretary for a law firm. So tell me, what did you guys do before you started riding around the country?"

"I was a lab-tech at a hospital in Portland," Kris said. "Jake was a designer at a manufacturing company that makes chain-saw blades, or something to that effect. I have a hard time keeping up with what he does. He tries to explain it to me, but it's just so much gibberish."

"Did you both just take a leave of absence?" Lisa asked.

"No," I said. "We really didn't know how long we would be gone, so we both quit our jobs. Kris was told she would be able to get hers back when she returned. I'll have to look for something new when we get back."

"Wow," Lisa said, "that's one gutsy move. Bob told me that you're riding from Oregon to Maine, which I don't understand at all! Whatever possessed you to do such a thing?"

Once again, we explained about the magazine article, and my wild hair. We spent the next couple days telling them about the people and sites we had seen so far. We also spent time finding out what was going on in their lives. After all, the last time I had seen them, they still lived in Wisconsin.

When we got ready to leave, Bob said to me, "I know you've driven across the Mississippi Bridge, but I wouldn't advise riding your bikes across it. There is a pedestrian lane, but it's all open grating. It will play havoc with your tires. So, why don't we take you over to Hudson, on the other side of the river?"

"Wow, that would be great," I said. "We were not looking forward to riding that bridge."

It happened to be a Saturday, so Bob and Lisa piled us into the van. However, we were not expecting them to take a side trip, to see the Capitol in St. Paul. It is a huge, magnificent building which houses the State Supreme Court, the Senate, and the House of Representatives. The Senate consists of 67 Senators, and the president of the Senate is elected by the members. The House has 134 members, and is presided over by the Speaker of the House. The House members elect him at the beginning of each legislative session. It is a position widely accepted to be the second most powerful position in the state government, behind the governor.

After the tour, we got back in the van and headed for Wisconsin.

Wisconsin

As we drove across the Mississippi River Bridge into Wisconsin, I pointed out to Kris what we would have been riding on. That open grating would have chewed up our tires. Once we cleared the bridge, Bob took the first exit and pulled in at a cafe. After we had lunch, we were ready to be on our way.

When we pulled out the bikes, Bob said, "By the way, you can't ride your bikes on the freeway. There is a frontage road that runs parallel to it, and you can use that."

"Thanks for the info," I said. "It was really nice seeing you guys again. We certainly enjoyed the hospitality."

"We are so glad that you stopped by." Lisa said. "I hope we can make it a little sooner next time. Hope you have a great trip, and God keep you safe."

After another round of hugs, we mounted our bikes, and waved as we took off down the road.

A little later on, we stopped at a drive-up information center. The lady in the booth asked where we were from, and we told her Oregon.

"Well," she replied, in a rather uppity tone of voice. "You certainly are a long way from O-ree-gon." Miss snooty looked over the top of her horn-rimmed glasses at our bikes, and continued, "Especially on those strange contraptions."

I was not real pleased with her attitude, so I asked, "Could you give us directions to You-Claire" (Eau Claire).

In a real uppity tone, she replied, "It is pronounced O-Claire."

I knew how to pronounce it, but I was trying to make a point. It must have been too obscure, because it sailed right over her pointed head.

A couple of days later we reached Wausau, which is about ninety miles east of Eau Claire. It had been a while since I had been back there, so, I called my brother Jim for directions to his house.

"You stay put right where you are," he told me. "I'm coming to get you."

Jim showed up about fifteen minutes later in his van (it seemed like everyone had a van), and we went through the introduction and hugging routine again. When we got to his house we were greeted by

Jim's wife, Candy, his two kids, and my dad. I introduced Kris, and then we all exchanged some tears and warm hugs.

Once that was over, I again had to explain our bikes. Of course, Jim's son and daughter wanted to try them out right away.

"Not right now," Jim told them. "You'll have plenty of time for that later." (We actually stayed for four days, so the kids had plenty of time to try out the bikes.)

Kris and I were able to spend a whole day with my dad, getting acquainted and reminiscing. Kris was just about rolling on the floor with laughter over some of the stories my dad was telling about me growing up. I was so embarrassed, and kept saying, "Dad, did you really have to tell her about that;" or "Come on, not that;" or "Oh my, I had totally forgotten about that."

And for you, the reader, I am *not* going to repeat those stories. But, it was all in good fun, and we had a great day.

The night before we left, my dad and brother put their heads together and threw a party for us. Many of my aunts, uncles, and cousins were there, and it was great to see them all again. Of course, Kris and I spent a lot of time talking about the trip, and about some of the people we had met.

At one point during the party, my cousin Sheila wandered over. "I think your trip is just amazing, but I would like to find out more about Oregon. I am a nurse, and about a week ago I got a call from a friend who works at one of the hospitals in Portland. She said they have an opening for a nurse, and would I be interested? I've been seriously considering it, and then you guys show up."

"What a coincidence," Kris said. "I used to work at a hospital as a lab-tech. What do you suppose the chances are of it being the same hospital?"

"That would be awesome," Sheila said. "I'm actually flying out there next week for an interview. My friend said that the Pacific Northwest is a great place to live. Is she right about that?"

"Well," I said, "we like to think so. The people are really nice, and the weather is a lot different. Due to an ocean current, it is much milder than it is here. During the winter, we occasionally get some snow, but it doesn't last long. However, we do get a lot of rain. I guess that's why it's so green."

"I think the summers are a lot like what you have here," Kris said. "That's when Jake and I usually head for the coast, where it's cooler. It's only a couple hours away, and we have our favorite bluffs that we go to. We like to watch the ocean waves roll in."

"I will definitely have to check that out," Sheila said.

When the party finally ended, we were pretty tired. Everyone wanted a chance to talk with us about the trip, and about Oregon, and we were happy to oblige.

The next morning my dad came over for a farewell breakfast. Afterward, we all said our goodbyes, and Kris and I were once again on our way.

A couple days later we pulled in to Marinette, on the border between Wisconsin and Michigan. This is another case of two cities separated by a river. In this case it was the Menominee River, which is also the state line. On one side of the river, in Wisconsin, it is called Marinette. On the other side, in Michigan, it is called Menominee. Both of them are situated on the shoreline of Green Bay. No, not the home of the Green Bay Packers NFL football team, but an actual body of water called Green Bay.

It's time for a little geography lesson. Place your left hand, *palm down,* on the table, on your leg, or somewhere. That is Wisconsin. Well, sort of. Now, do you see that space between your thumb and index finger? *That* is Green Bay. Don't know why it's called that, it just is.

Okay, enough with the geography lesson. Let's get back to the trip.

Michigan

That evening we crossed the bridge into Menominee, Michigan. We stayed at a quaint little motel that looked like it had come straight out of the fifties. It had neon lights around the windows, and the motel name was spelled out in red neon lights over the door.

Does it sound like we stayed in motels a lot? It turned out to be a lot more than we had originally planned. The enormous eruption of Mount St. Helens had seriously altered the weather patterns, and there was a lot more rain than usual. Sleeping in a real bed was a lot more comfortable than a sleeping bag in a soggy tent.

The next evening, as we followed the shoreline around the top of Lake Michigan, I ran into a bit of a problem. About two miles from the campground we had planned to stop at, I had a flat tire. No problem, just remove the tube and see if there was a thorn in the tire. Hmm, there was no thorn. I would have to check the tube later.

In the mean time, I put in a new tube, pumped up the tire, and we went on our way to the campground. After we had set up the tent, I noticed that the same tire was flat again. What was going on? Surely I must have a thorn in the tire, but there was not.

So what was it? I examined the first tube, and found two small holes very close together, which told me it was a rock pinch. When I thought back, I remembered riding through an area that had gravel on the road, and my tire went flat right after that.

The other tube had one little slit in it, so I must have pinched it when I installed it. Okay, get out the patch kit and fix both tubes. When that was done, I reinstalled one of the tubes and pumped up the tire. I was glad that was fixed.

Well, guess again Jake! The next morning, about a mile after we left the campground, Kris yelled to me that my tire was going flat. Not again! I figured that I must have pinched that stupid tube when I put it in. I was not happy as I sat down by the side of the road, and proceeded to *carefully* change tubes one more time. Thank goodness that was my last flat of the trip.

When we got started again, we continued to follow the Lake Michigan shoreline until we reached St. Ignace. That is the northern terminal of the Mackinac Bridge. The bridge connects the Lower and

Upper Peninsulas of Michigan. If you were to cross the bridge from south to north, Lake Huron would be on your right, and Lake Michigan would be on your left.

Out in Lake Huron, to the east of St. Ignace, we could see an island with some buildings on it. When Kris asked what it was, I told her that it was called Mackinac Island.

When I was growing up, I had always heard people talking about this interesting island in the straits of Mackinac. I had never had a chance to go there, so I was kind of excited to be able to do that.

We picked up a brochure in St. Ignace that said there are several miles of roads on the island, but there has *never* been a car accident. That's because cars are not allowed on the island. There are only horse-drawn carriages and bicycles, so we decided to take ours. You can reach the island by air, since it has its own airport, or you can take one of the many large ferries that service the island. We took the ferry.

There is a permanent population of about 600 on the island, so there are quite a few houses. There are also a number of hotels for visitors. The largest one, which you can see as you are approaching the island, is the Grand Hotel. It has 385 rooms, and no two are decorated the same. Rates start at $345 per day for a small single.

As I said, there are several miles of roads, and I think we rode them all. A lot of people had rented bicycles to tour the island. If some of those people drive their cars the way they rode those bikes, it is no wonder that we have so many accidents. They were not courteous, didn't watch where they were going, and they rode on the wrong side of the road.

At one point, I think *we* caused an accident. Well, not us exactly, it was our bikes. I noticed a guy riding toward us, looking at our bikes. He turned and continued to look as we went by, which caused him to turn his bike right into the path of another bike. Crash! They both went down in a heap. We stopped and I ran back to see if anyone was hurt. By the time I got there, both guys were on their feet, yelling at each other.

"Wait, wait" I yelled. They both stopped and looked at me. "Are you guys Okay?" They both nodded and picked up the bikes. I looked at both bikes and could not see any damage, but they both looked a little shaken. "Look" I said, "What happened was probably not his fault" as I pointed to the guy who had been watching us. His name turned out to be Gus, and the other one was Tim.

"But he turned right in front of me" argued Tim.

"Let me explain" I said. About this time Kris came walking back with our bikes.

"You know," Tim went on, "I saw you guys on those things in front of me, but I couldn't figure out what they were."

"Well, Gus had the same problem" I said, "and was watching us when he turned in front of you." By this time we had gathered some onlookers. "Until about a year ago, when we bought them, we didn't know what they were either. They are something new called recumbents, and they are very comfy. Go ahead, sit on them."

"You're sure it's Okay?" Gus asked, as he gingerly settled himself on mine. "Wow" he exclaimed, "you're absolutely right. This really puts that bike I'm riding to shame."

"Let me try" said Tim. He went over and sat on Kris's trike and his eyes lit up. "I see what you mean."

We talked a little more about the bikes, shook hands, and everyone continued on their way.

After visiting the island, we went back to the mainland to continue our journey. We were a little tired so we stayed that night in St. Ignace. The next day we traveled north to Sault St. Marie, and then crossed the bridge into Sault St. Marie. Now wait, don't get excited, I'll explain. We rode to Sault St. Marie, Michigan, and then crossed over the International Bridge into Sault St. Marie, Ontario. That's right, we crossed over into *Canada*!

CANADA

Ontario

THE INTERNATIONAL BRIDGE IS 2.8 miles long. It spans the Soo Locks on the Michigan side, and continues on across the St. Mary's River into Sault St. Marie, Ontario. Both the US and Canadian flags are mounted at the International Border in the middle of the bridge, along with a plaque showing the exact point of the International Border. We just had to stop and stand in two countries at once!

Things are a little different in Canada, eh! The license plates have a maple leaf on them, but then that's Canada, eh? Do you get my drift here, eh?

Now, don't get me wrong. I think that the way they end most of their sentences with *eh* is just a hoot, and it is part of the Canadian charm. It's just like *y'all* is part of our southern charm.

After crossing the International Bridge we had to go through Canadian customs. The customs agent was very gracious and had a few questions.

"What is the purpose of your visit, and your destination?" he asked.

"We're on a cross-country bike trip" I said, "and our destination is upstate New York."

He thanked us and continued, "Do you have any firearms?"

He probably figured that two people traveling cross-country on bicycles would definitely have a firearm, which we did not. All the while he was asking his questions, he kept glancing at our bikes. His final request was for us to open our bags. We were happy to oblige, as he was just doing his job to keep the borders safe.

After looking through our bags he said, "Everything looks fine and you are clear to continue. I have just one more question, off the record. What kind of bikes are those? I've never seen anything like them."

"They're something new in the way of bicycles," I said. "They're called recumbents. A bike builder in Oregon designed and built them for us. They are much more comfy than a standard bicycle."

"You said Oregon?" he asked. "You rode those things all the way from Oregon? What an adventure you two must be having. I would love to talk more about your trip, but I have a few other people waiting. Have a nice visit in Canada, and God bless."

Once we cleared customs we were on our way again, looking for Canadian Highway 17. That is the major Canadian highway that runs from the west coast to the east coast. Oh hey, we just found it, right where our map said it would be (duh). We rode the highway for a short way, until we came to a campground and stopped for the night.

After setting up camp and cleaning up, we took a walk around the campground. There were *lots* of U.S. travelers there, and we also found another cyclist. We went over to his campsite and introduced ourselves.

"Hi," I said. "I'm Jake and this is my wife, Kris. We're on a bike trip, and we're always on the lookout for fellow cyclists. Are you on a trip of some kind?"

Well," he said, "as a matter of fact I am. My name is Andrew, and I am doing an excursion across Canada on bicycle."

"Glad to meet you Andy," I said.

"If you don't mind" he replied, "I prefer Andrew." So, Andrew it was. "So tell me about your trip, eh?"

"Well, we started a couple months ago from Portland, Oregon" I replied. "Our destination is Portland, Maine."

"So, what are you doing in Canada, then?" he asked. "It seems to me that you would want to stay in the States."

"Riding south around the Great Lakes," I replied, "would take us through Chicago and the industrial areas of Indiana and Ohio. We agreed early on that we did not want to go through that area. So, here we are in Canada, going around the uncongested north side of the Great Lakes."

"That makes sense to me," Andrew said.

"So," Kris said, "tell us a little about your trip."

"Well," he began, "I wanted to make this trip for some time. I'm a college student back home, and next year I'll be a senior. After I graduate I'll have to go to work, so, this would be the last summer I could do this. A couple months ago I flew from Nova Scotia, where I live, to Vancouver, B.C. to begin my ride. It has been quite the experience, but I'm not real fond of the mountains. So, how are you folks getting along with the mountains?"

"Actually," Kris said, "they have turned out to be our favorite place to ride. Going up is kind of tough, but that ride down the other side is just exhilarating."

"Well now," Andrew responded, "I had never thought of it that way, but you are absolutely right. That ride down the back side is an absolute joy."

"Have you stayed in many motels?" I asked.

"Oh yes," he replied, "a lot more than I had intended to, thanks to that bloody volcano of yours."

We agreed, and had a good laugh about that "bloody volcano."

"When we got to Yellowstone," I told him, "we found out that we could have made a small fortune from all of that ash that we shoveled into garbage bags. They were selling little vials of that stuff for a buck."

Shortly thereafter, as Kris and I were preparing to leave, I asked Andrew if he would like to ride with us the next day.

"I would love to," he replied. "Thanks for the invitation."

With that we returned to our campsite and settled in for a good night's rest.

The next morning we rode over to Andrew's campsite and he just stood there with his mouth open.

"What in the world are you riding?" he asked. "Wait," he went on, "are those things recumbents?"

"They are indeed," I said.

"Wow," he said as he walked around our bikes. "I overheard someone at a bike shop talking about recumbents, and how comfortable they are. May I try it out?"

"Sure," I said. "Try mine."

He stepped over the low frame and gingerly sat down. I was holding the seat for him, and told him to lean back into the back rest.

As he did so, his eyes got bigger and he said, "You know what, they were right. This is really comfortable. I think you may have just ruined my trip. I'm not going to want to get back on my bike." He sat there for a moment and then said, "But, I guess I'll have to. You're certainly not going to let me ride this one."

We chuckled about that as we all mounted up and proceeded to ride on down the road.

Andrew was one of those people who didn't seem to get rattled easily. After a stop for pie and coffee that morning, we had a long, steep climb going out of the town. Kris and I were working our tails off, but Andrew just seemed to be taking a gentle afternoon ride. At the top of the grade we stopped for a drink, and his comment was, "Bit of a climb, eh," as if to say that it was no big deal. We just shook our heads and went on.

A few days later, we started seeing what appeared to be a chimney. As we got closer, that chimney got bigger, and taller. It turned out to be the Inco Superstack. It is 1,247 feet tall, and is the tallest freestanding chimney in the Western Hemisphere. It sits atop the world's largest nickel-smelting operation at Inco's Copper Cliff processing facility in the city of Sudbury. It was originally built in 1972 to disperse the sulphur gases of the smelting process away from the city.

However, that resulted in severe ecological damage in the area around Sudbury, which looked like a barren, rocky wasteland when we went through. Since then, the city has launched an ambitious rehabilitation plan, and has re-planted over three million new trees. Despite those efforts, much of the environmental damage to the area has turned out to be permanent. Much of the original pink-gray granite has been dyed jet black by the acid rain. A major construction effort has dramatically cleaned up the waste gases before they get pumped up the Superstack. Today, its primary exhaust is water vapor. When we went through, the sulfur smell was very prevalent.

Several days later, we stopped at a Provincial Park for the evening (I'll explain these later), and camped right next to us were two young ladies. They came over and introduced themselves as Jean and Sally. This may sound like a broken record, but they wanted to know about our weird bikes. I gave them our usual explanation, and then asked about them.

Jean said, "We're both from Vancouver, BC, and we're doing a cross-country trip in Sally's VW Beetle. We hope to end up somewhere in Nova Scotia. What about you folks, are you on a trip too?"

"Indeed we are," I said. "I'm Jake and this is my wife, Kris. We're from Portland, Oregon, and we're on our way to Portland, Maine. We met up with Andrew several days ago, and we've been riding together since."

"Hi ladies," he said, "my name is Andrew, and I'm a senior in college in Nova Scotia. A couple months ago, during my summer break, I flew to Vancouver and am now riding my bike back home." Both girls perked up when they found out that he was a single guy, and a fellow Canadian.

That evening, we all went to one of the nature programs that the park provides. After the program Kris and I went back to our campsite, but Andrew decided to stay up and chat with Jean and Sally. Surprise, Surprise! Kris and I figured that we had seen the last of Andrew as a traveling partner, and we couldn't blame him.

The next morning, as we were getting ready to break camp, Andrew came over and rather sheepishly said, "Thanks for allowing me to ride with you. Jean and Sally have asked me to ride along with them, and I have accepted their invitation. I've really enjoyed the time I spent with you, and hope the rest of your trip goes well." With that we shook hands and wished him a safe trip with the girls.

Here is a little more information about Ontario's 280 Provincial Parks. They have been developed, and are managed, by the Ontario Ministry of Natural Resources. The parks provide a variety of services, such as showers, flush toilets, trails and campsites. During the summer they have a variety of evening nature programs. They also have cabins and lodges for travelers to rent. We camped at a couple more Provincial Parks, and they were all clean and very hospitable.

After we left Andrew, we were kind of excited to see what experiences lay ahead of us. Every day we would make a couple stops for our usual pie and coffee. While in Canada, we noticed that they always served real cream with the coffee. Not half and half, or some non-dairy creamer, or milk, but *real* cream. Most of the time we just drank the coffee black, and then sipped on that delicious treat. We quickly became spoiled!

On one treacherous day, we had to ride five miles through a construction zone, before we were able to stop for lunch. Riding on gravel with fully loaded bicycles is hard work, and we were very relieved to get off the bikes and rest. But, we still had another twenty miles of construction ahead of us. But we were about to find out that we were in God's good graces that day. We were about halfway through our meal when a man walked over and introduced himself.

"Hi," he said. "I hope you'll forgive the interruption. My name is Dave. My wife Jennifer and I passed you as you were struggling to ride in here. We are just returning from dropping our daughter off at a college in Toronto, and are on our way home to Ottawa. We are driving a large empty van, and we were wondering if you would care to join us. That way you could bypass the next 20 miles of construction, and perhaps spend some time in Canada's capital city."

"That is a very kind gesture," I said, "especially since you don't know us."

I looked over at Kris and she nodded.

"We would love to," I told him. "Would you mind joining us while we finish our meal?" As Dave and Jennifer sat down I said, "I'm Jake and this is my wife, Kris."

They inquired about the bikes, and between bites we gave them our usual explanation. After we finished eating we loaded our bikes into their van.

It took us three hours to cover a distance that probably would have been a three-day ride. On the way to Ottawa, we gave them the whole story about my wild hair, and some of our experiences along the way. They were all ears.

When we reached their home, on the outskirts of Ottawa, they invited us to stay for dinner.

"Thank you very much," Kris said. "We would be happy to join you."

Jennifer scurried off to the kitchen, and we joined Dave in the living room. I could see that he had something on his mind, and he finally said, "I assume that you had planned to go to a campground or a motel tonight. Would you care to stay here for the night? Since our daughter is gone, we have an empty bedroom." He noticed that we were a bit hesitant. "If you're concerned about the bikes, we can lock them up in the garage."

"It is not about the bikes," I replied. "It's just that you've been overly generous already, and we don't want to put you out."

"Let me explain about the generosity," he said. "A few years back, we were helped out with an anonymous donation of a kidney for our daughter. Ever since then, if we are able to help someone else out, we do so. That being the case, would you be willing to accept our offer?"

We were overwhelmed, and did indeed accept their offer. Not only did they provide us with a place to stay, but Jennifer had whipped up a delicious meal of spaghetti and meatballs. After dinner, they told us a little about themselves. Jennifer was a nurse at a local hospital, and Dave was an engineer at a manufacturing company. Kris and Jennifer started comparing notes, since Kris had been a lab-tech before we left. Dave and I were able to compare notes also, since I had been a designer at a manufacturing company before the trip.

When Kris and I started to run down, they showed us to their daughter's room, which had an attached bathroom. As I said, I think we were in God's good graces that day.

The next morning, after a hearty breakfast of pancakes and eggs, we got the bikes out of the garage, and were getting ready to leave.

Dave handed me a map and said, "Since you have never been here before, here is a map of Ottawa. One the attractions that we recommend you should see is the changing of the guard at the Parliament Building. We've been to see it several times, and it's quite impressive. We've really enjoyed having you here, and we wish you well on the rest of your journey."

Ottawa

Since we were in the Capital city of Canada, we decided to play tourist. We rode around for a little while, and then got a motel room for several days. That way we would have a place to leave our bikes while we rented a car.

So, what did we want to see first? Since it was the capital, why not go see the capitol building. In Ottawa's case it turned out to be the Parliament Building. It is situated on what they call Parliament Hill. This huge building houses both the Senate chamber and the House of Commons chamber.

The Senate Chamber was at the east end of the building, and the House of Commons Chamber is at the west end of the building. The Senate Chamber had red carpeting, red upholstery, and a ceiling of gold leaf. At the north end of the chamber sat three large chairs. (Actually, there was a throne and two stately looking chairs.) They were arranged with one chair in front for the Speaker of the Senate, and the throne and the other chair situated behind the Speaker on a raised platform. When the Queen of England is in attendance, for the opening of Parliament, she sits on the throne and her consort sits next to her. When she is not in attendance, the Governor General takes her place. The Senators sit at red upholstered desks on either side of the center aisle.

The House of Commons Chamber was decorated in green in the tradition of the British House of Commons. The ceiling was made of softly colored linen canvas, and painted with symbols from coats of arms. Stained-glass windows depicted the floral emblems of Canada's provinces and territories. The Speaker's chair was at the north end of the Chamber. Members of the Government sit on the benches to the Speaker's right, while members of the Opposition occupy benches on the Speaker's left. Government ministers sit around the Prime Minister, who is traditionally assigned the 11th seat in the front row, on the Speaker's right.

We spent most of the day at Parliament Hill before returning to our motel. The next morning we drove over to Parliament Hill to watch a Canadian tradition: the ceremonial Changing of the Guard. That takes place every morning during the summer months. The guards march through the streets of Ottawa from their barracks, arriving at

Parliament Hill at precisely 10:00 am. The thirty-minute ceremony consisted of music and complex precision marching by the guards. As Dave said, it was quite spectacular.

The following morning we were, as Willie Nelson would say, on the road again. This time, we were headed toward the good old USA. We rode south to Morrisburg, which is right along the St. Lawrence Seaway. We could look across the water and see the USA on the other side, but we were not able to cross over at that point. We had to ride south along the seaway for another 22 miles to Prescott, before we came to a border crossing.

Back in the USA

New York State

Aᴛᴛᴇʀ ᴄʀᴏssɪɴɢ ᴛʜᴇ ʙʀɪᴅɢᴇ back into the USA, and doing our customary high five, we had to go through customs again. The US customs officer we were working with asked us most of the same questions that we had to answer when we entered Canada.

"Do you have any fruit that you purchased in Canada?" He asked.

We did not.

"Do you have any weapons?"

Once again, we did not.

"Are you United States citizens?"

Yes, we were. We had to show him our Oregon driver's license.

"I'm sorry, but I'm going to have to ask you to empty all of our bags," he said.

I guess they had to be sure we weren't smuggling anything. We were happy to oblige, since he was just doing his job. We were rather surprised that he didn't say anything about the bikes. But then, it was a rather busy time and there were other people lined up behind us.

After re-packing our bags, we continued on our way into Ogdensburg, New York. The time we spent in Canada was fun, and the people were great, but it was sure nice to be back in our own country.

That evening we stopped at a small café for dinner. When we asked for a refill on our coffee, the waiter picked up our check and added two more coffees to the bill. What? Everywhere else, even in Canada, a second cup had been offered at no charge. Oh well, every café and restaurant had its own way of doing things.

We spent several days traveling through upstate New York. The beautiful trees and farmlands reminded us very much of Oregon, or perhaps Wisconsin.

A few days later we rode into the city of Champlain, named after the large lake it is situated next to, and took a room at a motel.

Most of Lake Champlain, one of our largest freshwater lakes, is located within the borders of the United States, and part of it is located in the Canadian province of Quebec. Several Revolutionary War battles were fought a little further south at Fort Ticonderoga.

The lake is also reported to have its own sea monster, called Champ. Some authorities regard Champ as a legend. Others believe that such a creature, possibly a relative of the Loch Ness Monster, does indeed live deep in the lake. While there is no scientific evidence of its existence, there have been more than three hundred reported sightings.

There are only two roads that cross Lake Champlain. One is near the southern end of the lake, and the other is at the northern part of the lake. Fortunately for us, the northern crossing is at the city of Champlain. A large bridge crosses part of the lake onto a large island called Grand Isle, which, technically, is in Vermont.

Vermont

The next morning we crossed the bridge onto Grand Isle. After riding a short way we turned south onto Hwy 2, also known as the Theodore Roosevelt Hwy.

At the southern end of Grand Isle we crossed a short bridge onto North Hero Island. The road took us to the east side of the island along the shoreline of Lake Champlain. At the south end of the island we crossed another bridge onto *South* Hero Island.

We continued to head south until the highway curved east around Keeler Bay. In front of us was yet another bridge, which took us off the island and into Vermont.

We followed Hwy 2 for about ten miles into Burlington, Vermont and found a motel for the evening.

The next day we again followed Hwy 2 until we reached Montpelier, the State Capital. While doing some sightseeing, we came across a Bed and Breakfast and decided to investigate. Doreen, the lady who owned the place, said she had a room available and a secure shed to park our bikes. That sounded like a good deal, so we took it.

She took us around to a garage behind the large colonial house. Her car was parked there, but we still had plenty of room for our bikes. We brought our bags with us and Doreen showed us to our room on the second floor. The only bathroom was located down the hall. We happened to be the only ones there that night, so Doreen asked us to join her and her ten year old daughter, Sharon, for dinner. She served up pork chops, mashed potatoes, corn, and a luscious green salad. What a delicious treat.

After dinner she invited us into the living room for coffee.

"I usually don't like to pry," she said, "but my curiosity had gotten the better of me. What do you call those things you are riding? I mean, they are not exactly bicycles, and yet they are, most curious."

"They are called *recumbent* bicycles," I replied.

"Are they something new?" she asked. "I've never seen anything like them. Of course, we don't have much of a chance to keep up on new things. Most of our time is spent right here."

"Yes," I said, "they are somewhat new. A bicycle builder back home designed and built them for us. They are way more comfortable than the standard bicycles."

"They sure looked like it. You said back home," she inquired. "Just where might that be?"

"Actually," Kris said, "we are from Portland, Oregon."

"You meant Maine, didn't you?" she asked. "Portland, Maine? I thought I heard you said Oregon."

Kris grinned and replied, "Yes, I did say Oregon. And yes, we did ride them all this way."

"That is just amazing." Doreen replied. "You two must be having quite an adventure."

"We are indeed," I said. I went on to explain about my wild hair, and about some of the people and places we had seen along the way.

"Oh my," Doreen said as she got kind of a far-away look in her eye. "My husband would have loved to sit and talk with you about your trip. He so enjoyed traveling and adventure."

"Oh?" Kris asked.

"Yes," she said, "he died in Viet Nam in 1970. His parents gave us this house so we could set up a bed and breakfast. We had been in business for a couple years when he got drafted, and I was pregnant with Sharon when he left. When we heard the news of Bob's death, his folks came and stayed with me, because I was quite a mess. Bob's dad took over the business, and his mom was a Godsend when the baby arrived. I would not have made it without them. They still treat me as if I were their real daughter. I feel truly blessed"

We chatted for a little while longer before Kris and I decided to call it a day.

The next morning we went out to explore Montpelier, the smallest State Capital in the United States. Our B&B was situated fairly close to the downtown area, so we were able to walk wherever we wanted to go.

Our first stop was the Capitol Building. The original building burned down in 1857, and a new building was built on the same spot in 1859. It houses the Representatives Hall and the Senate Chamber, both of which are on the second floor. The Representative's Hall is home to the 150-member House of Representatives, and it has been restored to the way it looked in 1859. Directly behind the Speaker's rostrum hangs a historic portrait of George Washington. It was rescued from the fire that destroyed the original statehouse.

The Senate Chamber, with all its original furnishings, is remarkably well preserved. With only 30 members, the Chamber is an intimate, yet grand room. It had a magnificent gasolier, (a gas-fired chandelier) that had been found and reinstalled after an absence of nearly 65 years.

We spent two days visiting the Capitol and some of the shops in Montpelier. While we were getting our bikes ready to leave, Doreen and her daughter fixed us a delicious breakfast of scrambled eggs, bacon and toast. She wished us well on the rest of our journey, and handed us a snack for later on down the road (another nice gesture).

Our original plan had been to head south and then east around the White Mountains. However, Doreen had told us that we could not go around those mountains. They are part of a larger chain called the Appalachian Mountains. So, rather than add extra miles by heading south, we decided to head east and brave the mountains one more time by riding through the White Mountains National Forest.

It seemed as if the distance we were riding each day was getting shorter. Perhaps we were slowing down to admire the beautiful forest scenery. However, since we were getting closer to our destination, maybe we were just trying to stretch things out. Whatever the reason, after a short ride of only forty miles, we stopped one more time in Vermont at a town called St. Johnsburg. The next morning, after having breakfast at a small café, we rode on into New Hampshire.

New Hampshire

New Hampshire had the same beautiful scenery of deciduous trees and bubbling streams as we had seen in Vermont. But, there was a little surprise waiting for us. After a short climb, the road leveled out in a heavily wooded area. As we were riding along, a female moose came out of the woods and crossed the road about fifty yards in front of us. We had both seen pictures of moose, but that did not prepare us for how big she was.

This particular lady stood about six feet high at the shoulder, almost tall enough for us to ride right under her. When we got to the point where she had crossed the road, we saw her standing at the edge of the woods, watching us. Kris decided she needed a picture, so she stopped and snapped off a couple of shots.

The click of the shutter must have startled the moose, because she started walking toward us. We took off as fast as our little legs could pedal, but now she was following us. When she came back onto the road behind us, she stopped and watched as we rode away from her. We breathed a sigh of relief and continued on down the road.

The mountains of New Hampshire did not provide any more surprises, so we were able to slow down and enjoy the scenery. We rode through some thickly forested areas, and some cleared areas with several houses and outbuildings. That evening we stopped at a campground close to a smooth running stream. As the sun was setting we noticed how the water was as smooth as glass. There were puffy white clouds reflected in the still water, and it looked as if nature had painted a special picture for us.

The next day we followed that stream for several miles. We seemed to be in a wonderland with the stream beside us, and a forest all around us. We finally lost sight of the stream when the road turned and we started climbing through the forest. It was very pleasant until the forest cleared and we came to a sharp curve in the road. There was a guard rail that went around the curve, and we could not see anything on the other side except a valley far below. We both got off our bikes and walked until the road straightened out again. It was just too scary being that close to the edge.

Surprisingly, climbing that pass, and several others, was a lot easier than we had expected. The mountains in New Hampshire were not nearly as high, nor the roads as steep, as what we had experienced in the Rockies. But the wooded scenery was much prettier than the rocky terrain of the west.

Late that afternoon, after finishing an early dinner in Conway, we got back on our bikes and headed for Maine.

Maine

We were both kind of excited about being so close to our destination, but it was still a full day's ride away. So, we stopped at a small town just over the border that had a very inviting Bed and Breakfast. Since we had such a good experience in Vermont, we decided to give it another shot.

Ken, the owner, greeted us as we signed in. He took us around back to his garage where we were able to lock up the bikes for the night. Of course, he wanted to know all about the bikes and our trip. We spent several hours talking with him about our trip and the different people we had met. When we started getting drowsy, he showed us to our room. The next morning we were greeted with a delicious breakfast of pancakes and eggs. After Ken wished us well, we were on our way again.

Our trip had taken us through thirteen states, the Canadian Province of Ontario, and the Canadian Capital of Ottawa. Quite the little excursion!

Along the way, to our final stop of Portland, Maine, we noticed that there were huge fields of low bushes that had a bluish hue to them. At our next stop for pie and coffee, we asked the waitress about those bushes.

"Those are blueberries," she said, "which are a very big cash crop here. You are obviously not from here or you would know that. So where are you from?"

"We are actually from Portland, Oregon" Kris told her.

"Oregon?" she asked. "But you have bicycle helmets. Next, you are going to tell me you rode bicycles all that way."

"We sure did," Kris replied, "and we're getting very close to our destination of Portland, Maine."

The waitress just stood there with her mouth open. "No way!" she exclaimed. "Are you serious? You really rode bicycles all that way?" She hesitated for a moment and said, "Don't go away," and scurried off.

She was back in just a minute with her manager in tow.

"This is Don, my boss" she said, all excited. "Would you mind telling him about your trip?" She turned to Don and said, "They said they rode bicycles all the way from Portland, Oregon."

Don sat down and we introduced ourselves. "Sherry tends to get a little excited, as you can see," he said. "But then, you two are something to get excited about." He noticed that Sherry was still standing there. "Sherry," he said, "tell Linda to take over your tables and then come sit down."

He didn't have to tell her twice; she hurried off and was back in just a minute.

We talked with them for about a half hour. We told them about my wild hair, what states we had been through, about going into Canada, and finally about the terrific people we had met along the way. They were both enthralled, especially Sherry.

When we finally decided to leave, Don told us not to worry about the check, it was his treat. It was another one of those nice gestures that we had run into so many times before.

As we headed on down the road, and got closer to Portland, we were getting more and more excited. When we finally reached the Portland city limits sign, I turned to Kris and said, "Can you believe it? That sign says Portland, Maine! We're almost there." We were both so excited that we could hardly contain ourselves.

Before we started this amazing trip, we had dipped our rear wheels in the Pacific Ocean. Now we wanted to dip our front wheels into the Atlantic Ocean, but we had no idea how we were going to do that. When we looked in our bags for our map of Portland, it was not there. Evidently we had forgotten to include it when we were packing. So, we stopped at a convenience store to get another one. As I was paying for it, I asked the lady at the counter if she could show me the best place to get down to the water. She pointed out a beach that was fairly easy to get to that would serve our purpose.

So, with map in hand, we were once again on our way. We rode around a bit before heading down to the water. I guess we wanted to prolong things a bit. When we finally got to the spot where we could actually get down to the water, we stopped on the walkway above the beach, and looked out on the Atlantic Ocean. The beautiful blue water seemed to just draw us in.

A man walking by finally broke the spell, when he asked, "Isn't that a beautiful sight?"

"Indeed it is," I replied as he walked on.

"Well," Kris said, "we're finally here. Shall we head down there?"

"Just a minute," I replied. "I want to take this all in first."

"Jake," she said, "you're stalling again."

"Okay, okay" I said. "Let's do it."

We followed the walkway down to the beach, and rolled our bikes across the sand to the edge of the water. When the surf of the Atlantic Ocean lapped over onto our front wheels, the excitement we were feeling bubbled over into a yell of "Yahoo, we made it." We were laughing and crying as we did a little dance around the bikes.

Quite a few of the people on the beach were curiously watching our little display. Of course, they had no idea of what had just taken place. We were celebrating the completion of the trip of our lives, riding our bikes from the Pacific Ocean to the Atlantic Ocean.

As we were walking our bikes back off the beach, something dawned on us. Okay, our amazing adventure was complete, so now what? We had originally planned to ride down to Virginia for the winter, and then ride back to Oregon the following spring on the Bikecentenial Trail. However, that plan fell apart in Idaho when Kris developed sore knees. Guess it was time to find a place where we could talk things over. On our way to a motel, we passed a used car lot that had the *cutest* little blue Honda …

"Jacob," Kris shouted to me, "did you see that cute little car back there?"

"You mean that little blue one?" I asked.

"That's the one," she replied. "It seemed like it was calling to us. Should we go back and check it out?"

We looked at each other, snickered, and made a quick u-turn. After three months of riding across the country, we were ready for something different.

But … that's another story!

APPENDIX

About Recumbent Bicycles

YOU MAY HAVE SEEN them, those odd shaped bicycles that have more in common with lawn furniture than a typical bicycle. I'm referring to *Recumbent Bicycles*, those sit-down bikes that are pedaled with your feet out in front of you.

Recumbent bikes have actually been around since the late 1800's. During the 1930's the racing community banned them from any further competitions, because they were faster than standard bicycles. That pretty much killed the recumbent design until the early 1970's, when some bicycle designers started tinkering with them again. Out of this came some new designs that were comfy, handled well, and they were fairly fast. Today there are quite a few manufacturers of quality recumbents.

All recumbents use a seat that is much like an office chair. The seat bottom is usually padded, with a mesh back rest to lean against. This tends to give you a very comfortable ride.

The two most common recumbent bicycles, based on where the front wheel is located, are the short-wheelbase and the long-wheelbase.

- The short-wheelbase bike has the front wheel located right under the knees, with the pedals located out in front. This configuration has a fairly stiff ride and quick handling as you are sitting very close to the front wheel.

- The long wheelbase bike is more stretched out, with the pedals located behind the front wheel. This gives you a much softer ride, but has a much larger turning radius than the short wheelbase.

NOT JUST BICYCLES

Not all recumbents are bicycles. Some of them are tricycles, which appeals more to riders who have balance problems. There are two different tricycle designs.

- Tadpole

  This design has two wheels in front and one wheel in back. It is much like the short wheelbase bike design in that the front wheels are located just outside of the knees, and the pedals are located out in front. This design tends to have a much lower seat, often about a foot above the pavement.

- Delta

  This design has one wheel in front and two wheels in back. It tends to be more like the long wheelbase bike, since the pedals are located behind the front wheel.

The longer delta tricycle usually has a much smaller turning radius than the tadpole. The tadpole design steers both of the front wheels, much like a car, but cannot turn as sharply as you can with the single front wheel of the delta design.

Just a few statistics:

- We started on June 1, 1980 and finished on August 28, 1980

- We averaged about 54 miles a day

- The trip was about 3,700 miles

- We each wore out two rear tires and one front tire

- Kris had one flat tire, and I had three

- Neither of us had any mechanical failures

Notes

By taking a northern route, and going through Canada and the New England states, we avoided the hustle and bustle of the more populated areas. Seeing this country of ours, and our neighbor to the north, at a slower pace was really fantastic. It allowed us to see, and really observe, a myriad of spectacular scenery.

But, you know what made this trip so amazing? It was the wonderful people we met. Many of them took a little time to chat with us about our journey and our experiences. Perhaps our story may have given someone the courage, or maybe that little nudge, that they needed to go out and experience their own amazing journey.

Capital or Capitol

Throughout this trip I've used the words *capital* and *capitol*.
They look the same, right? Aha, but they're not!
The word "capit**a**l," spelled with an A, refers to a city.
The word "capit**o**l," spelled with an O, refers to a building.

Here is how I keep them straight:
Capital with an A is a pl**A**ce,
Capitol with an O is a h**O**use.

Kind of silly, but it works for me.

Lessons Learned

- If you have a goal, or something to shoot for, the work gets easier the more you do it.

- No matter how good or how bad the conditions – on a bicycle or in life – you just have to keep on keepin' on.

- Appreciate the tough times, such as riding in the rain or climbing a steep mountain pass. (I didn't say we liked them, we just learned to appreciate them.) Those experiences were just preparing us to really enjoy the good times, such as a sunny day or the long downhill on the other side of the mountain. We always called them our "Reward."

- If we thought about the long mountain climb we had in front of us, it could be rather intimidating. But if we thought about just making it to the next bend in the road, it suddenly got easier. And so it is with life. If you focus on small goals, the long journey to your destination becomes that much easier.

- No matter what you attempt to do, there will always be those who do it better. Just do the best that *you* can, and try not to compare yourself to others. They may have skills that you have yet to learn.

When we reached Portland, Maine, our amazing adventure had ended. However, we had accumulated a wealth of experiences that we would remember for the rest of our lives!

So, here is our advice:

Strive for that goal, but *ENJOY THE JOURNEY*

There is so much fun to be had

There are so many lessons to be learned

ALONG THE WAY